THE GIRL WHO VANQUISHED THE DRAGON

James Warwood

(Starring a village full of animals who need rescuing from a Dragon Overlord, also poop, the Sandwich Sandwich shop (owned by a zebra), rabbit poop, four horseraddishes, lion poop, a knight in shining armour, penguin poop, a girl called Penny, mouse poop, Mr Fitz's Fabulous Formula, gorilla poop, a cardboard box, elephant poop, and lots and lots and lots and lots and lots and lots of lasagne.)

THE GIRL WHO VANQUISHED THE DRAGON

Previous Title: The Village Creatures

Produced by Curious Squirrel Press
Paperback ISBN: 978-1-915646-12-5
Ebook ASIN: B083TJHGFD

Cover art & illustrations by James Warwood
Edited by Rachel Mann
Interior design by James Warwood

www.cjwarwood.com

Give feedback on the book at:
me@cjwarwood.com

Second Edition

for Rebecca & Reuben,
my two favourite R's in the world

1

NOTHING EVER HAPPENS

There once was a quaint little village on the south-east coast of England called Sandwich.

Yep, no need to reread the last sentence. You read it correctly.

This story is not about a village town like Suttonfield or Great Whittington or Llanfairpwllgwyngyllgogerych-wyrndrobwllllantysiliogogogoch (a lovely village in Wales whose name roughly translates as "the church in the valley of fluffy unicorns next to a muddy puddle owned by St Bob the Third, king of all the ginger biscuits").

There was a real place called Sandwich, and if you read on, I'd be delighted to tell you more about it.

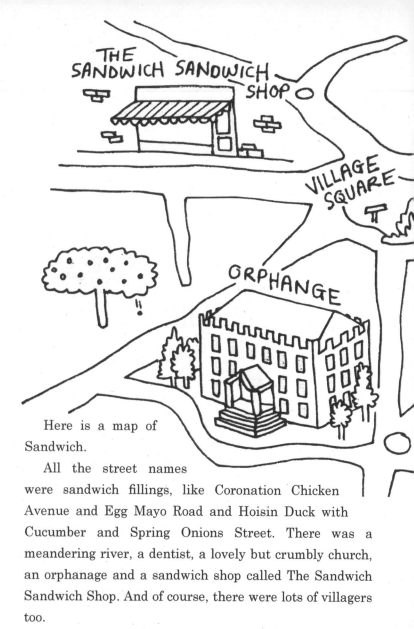

THE SANDWICH SANDWICH SHOP

VILLAGE SQUARE

ORPHANGE

Here is a map of Sandwich.

All the street names were sandwich fillings, like Coronation Chicken Avenue and Egg Mayo Road and Hoisin Duck with Cucumber and Spring Onions Street. There was a meandering river, a dentist, a lovely but crumbly church, an orphanage and a sandwich shop called The Sandwich Sandwich Shop. And of course, there were lots of villagers too.

If you could imagine a sandwich filling, Mrs Wrinklebottom would make it for you. For example, you could ask her for a tuna sandwich, and she would reply,

SANDWICH
CHURCH

DENTIST

"The
fish, or
a snack while
I sing 'Baa

Baa Black Sheep'?" Mrs Wrinklebottom looked and smelt like she had sampled all the fillings in her shop, including the out-of-date ones.

Mr Dickens suffered from cross-eye syndrome. Everything he saw had a nose in the way, his nose to be precise. The poor man also had a shaky hand, believed ghosts lived in his cupboard and had an irrational fear of being licked by small children. So, naturally, he became the village dentist, partly because it paid well but mostly because nobody else wanted to do it.

Every Sunday morning, Reverend Nightingale began her sermon with the words "Lettuce play." This was because a) her favourite sandwiches were lettuce sandwiches, and it amused her, as it sounded like let us, and b) she struggled to pronounce her r's. Her congregation did not mind, as they were all asleep anyway, tucked up in their homes, having a lovely lie-in.

In the orphanage sat one lonely child. She was the only orphan in the whole of Sandwich. And to make matters even worse, the orphanage was a massive old stately home with hundreds of dusty old rooms. It was the perfect place to play hide-and-seek, but only if you had someone to play with.

Nothing ever happened in Sandwich. Believe me, more interesting stuff happens in your maths teacher's pencil case. It was the most boring place in the whole world. So much so that a plaque had been put up in the village square that read "On 29 March 1918, in this spot, nothing happened."

And so the people of Sandwich carried on with their boring lives, eating strange sandwiches and not doing anything of any significance. As always, nothing happened for the next one thousand years, and that was that.

THE END

(Oh, wait . . . there was this one thing, and that's what this story is all about. Silly me!)

It all started to go wrong when Mr Fitz came to visit.

2

MR FITZ
AND HIS SUITCASE OF
FABULOUS FORMULAS

"Roll up! Roll up!"

A confused villager heard the command and rolled up his sleeves.

The travelling salesman chuckled, "That's not what I meant, me duck." Mr Fitz put down his suitcase and shouted a bit louder. "Come on, you lazy slobs, don't be shy. Roll up! I ain't gonna say it again."

The village folk were a simple but curious bunch. Nothing interesting or noteworthy ever happened in their neighbourhood. So, naturally, they were the nosiest people in the whole world. A crowd began to form around the out-of-towner and his mysterious suitcase.

"Inside my marvellous suitcase I've got potions, lotions and ointments for every ailment under the sun. For example, this miraculous cream," said the salesman as he picked up a small brown tin from his suitcase, "will cure any kind of ache."

"Will it cure my headache?" asked a scruffy-looking villager.

"Of course."

"What about my backache?" asked another villager.

"Yes indeed, and your frontache too."

"Surely it couldn't cure my tooth-, ear- and bellyache," scoffed someone at the back.

"Oh, yes, it could," he replied with a smile. "And it would cure all three quicker than a rocket-fuelled rat wearing rollerblades."

The crowd mumbled with interest. Mr Fitz felt their excitement bubbling, and so he kicked it up a notch. "Or is it the undesirable smells from behind that ail you? Then fear not, as only here in my suitcase will you find the antidote." The skinny man, dressed in a purple velvet suit, picked up a green bottle and held it high for all to see. "Uncle Pete's Anti-Gas reacts with your stomach acids, preventing the process during which food turns into unpleasant gas. In just one week, you'll be trumping daisies, guaranteed."

The crowd grew bigger and bigger. Everyone wanted to see what else was inside the suitcase. Toes were stepped on and beards were pulled, and backbones were used as makeshift stepladders. No one cared, as long as they could see the next shiny-looking object being lifted upward.

"But, ladies and gentlemen, you'll be pleased to hear that I have saved the best till last."

Mumblings and mutterings spread across the crowd like jam on a warm crumpet. What could possibly be better? Everyone in the whole village was now standing in the village square, hanging on the salesman's every word.

"Do you suffer from tiredness, paleness, coughs, a runny nose, aches and pains, hair loss, fevers and chills? According to the quacks with fancy university degrees, all such ailments are symptoms of the common cold. They also claim it to be incurable. Well, after years of painstaking research, I have perfected a medicine." He then reached down and opened his suitcase, revealing hundreds of little clear glass bottles (and if you had the time to count them, you would notice that there was one bottle for every

villager).

"I call it Mr Fitz's Fabulous Formula. Not only does it cure you of the common cold for the rest of your natural life, it also reinvigorates your vitality, increases your intelligence and even restores your hair." He turned to look at a man in the crowd, who blushed while rubbing his smooth head. "I myself used to be a bald cripple with a cough that could deafen the neighbour's cat, but look at me now! As I like to say, whatever you've got, it'll cure the lot. Now come and get it while stocks last."

The crowd rushed forward with shiny silver and gold coins at the ready. Everyone wanted to get their mitts on the formula, except for one inquisitive little girl.

"Excuse me," the girl asked politely, "but aren't you supposed to say 'Any questions?' at the end?"

"No, no, young lady," said Mr Fitz as he exchanged bottles for coins. "You're confusing me with a teacher or a plumber. I'm a salesman, and everyone knows you can trust a salesman. We're honest folk." The sides of his mouth awkwardly curled upward like a caterpillar doing a sit-up.

"But I've got a question."

"Well, I'm a little busy at the moment, kid."

"It's just that there is a lot of tiny writing on the label of your formula. Why does it have to be so small? I can hardly read it."

Mr Fitz froze and began to sweat all over. "Read it? I thought none of you country folk could read."

The people in earshot laughed. "You can ignore Penny," explained a happy customer. "She loves reading and writing and all that educational stuff, but she's the only one. The rest of us can't even read our own names." The villager then took a hearty swig of the formula. "Amazing, I can feel it working already."

"Thank the heavens," sighed the sweaty salesman. "That, my dear, is what we in the business call the 'small print'. All the bona fide medicines have them. That's how you can tell they're the real deal. As I always say, the smaller the print the better the product."

"Oh," said Penny. "I suppose that makes sense. And what about these funny little symbols? This one that shows an upside-down rat with its feet in the air and an x where its eye should be is a bit worrying. Wouldn't you agree?"

Her question floated away with no reply. The salesman had just sold his last bottle and vanished into thin air. The crowds began to disperse, each one pleased with their new purchase, as they happily glugged down the formula. Every last drop.

Well, everyone except for Penny.

3

EARL

Penny skipped home after her unusual morning. She was excited.

For the first time in her life, something had happened in her village, and she was clutching a bottle containing it.

The bouncy girl was a proud Sandwicheerian (which is what you call someone who lives in Sandwich or someone who eats far too many sandwiches). Her parents used to live in Sandwich. Her grandparents used to live in Sandwich. In her opinion, it was the best place in the whole world, and the Queen should put Buckingham Palace up for sale and move in next door.

Penny noticed that everyone she passed was glugging Mr Fitz's Fabulous Formula like a can of fizzy pop. They pulled all sorts of funny faces as they gulped. Some looked as though a hippopotamus had sat on their big toe. Others looked as though a hedgehog had settled down for a nap in their underwear.

She skipped past *The Sandwich Sandwich Shop*. It was full of customers looking for the perfect lunch. What could she smell this morning? Was it baked beans? Was it Brussels sprouts? Or was it blue cheese (a wonderful ingredient that is highly stinky and only slightly toxic)? The most likely answer was that it was all three happily mingling together inside a freshly baked brown bap.

"Hello, Mrs Wrinklebottom," said Penny.

"Hello, Penny," said Mrs Wrinklebottom. She was stood behind her shop counter and was slurping her bottle through a straw.

She skipped past Sandwich Church. It was an impressive building with a big stone spire and a large stone graveyard and a long stone wall surrounding it. Reverend Nightingale was playing badminton with her favourite member of her congregation. It was a very one-sided match, as Mrs Pratt was now dead and under a tombstone, and therefore struggled to hold her racket.

"Hello, Reverend Nightingale," said Penny.

"Hello, Penny," said the minister as she took a refreshing swig of Mr Fitz's Fabulous Formula.

She skipped past the dentist. To most, it would look like a very normal-looking house. However, Penny knew it was the dentist, because of the sounds of low-pitched boredom, medium-pitched drilling and very high-pitched screaming. That and the big sign, which was a giveaway. Outside stood a glass recycling bin full of empty glass bottles.

She turned the corner and instantly recognised where she was – Cornish Pasty Lane.

She skipped towards a well-used cardboard box. A pair of hairy legs that belonged to Earl stuck out of the box. He didn't have a house. He didn't have a job. He didn't even have any socks or shoes or sandwiches for that matter. The people of Sandwich had become very good at pretending he didn't exist. But he didn't care, because he still had his words.

"Sharpen me nose and call me a swordfish! It's my good friend Penny."

"Hi, Earl. You'll never guess what happened in the village square this morning."

"Erm, nothing?"

"Nope," smiled Penny. "In fact, quite the opposite. Something happened."

Earl zapped into the air and landed in the handstand position. "Lick me kneecaps and call me a lollypop!"

Penny explained exactly what had happened. About the salesman and his suitcase and the bottles of formula that everyone had bought. And the more she explained, the redder his face became (because he

PENNY

(the village orphan)

was still doing a handstand).

"Well, pick the fleas outta me armpits and call me a chimpanzee!"

Penny laughed. She knew this was the way Earl liked to talk, so she did not reach for his armpits or call him a chimpanzee. If she did, then she would probably lose her fingers to gangrene.

"I was wondering what all these bottles were for." Earl waved his leg towards the pile of bottles he had collected. "And now that I know they had the formula inside, I shall crack one open and lick it until it's as clean as a whistle."

Earl walked on his hands over to the pile of bottles and grabbed the closest one. Just as he was about to dribble a drop of formula onto his upside-down tongue, a stray dog leaped into the air and knocked the bottle out of his hand. The bottle flew through the air and smashed into a million pieces.

"Oi! What did you do that for?"

"Hey, don't shout at Buster. He stopped you from doing something

EARL
(the village idiot)

stupid."

Buster wagged his tail.

"Oh. Sorry, my hairy chum. I'm lucky to have friends as clever as you and Buster."

Penny giggled because she knew it was true. Buster was a very intelligent dog. He was the only stray dog in the village, much like Penny was the only orphan in the village. Earl loved him because he would keep him company when the nights turned cold and share his scraps of leftover sandwiches with him. Penny loved him because he was always so happy to see her. He was the kind of dog she always wished she would have if she had a normal family.

"I don't think the formula is very safe," said Penny as she patted Buster and picked up the bottle of formula in her pocket. "See, look at this little symbol on the bottle," explained Penny as she held up her bottle to Earl.

Earl inspected the symbol and said, "Ahhhhh, look, the little rat is having a lovely little nap."

"Well, I think the rat is having a not-so-lovely death. And just look at all the small print on the back. I don't think a formula should have words on it like 'dangerous' and 'caution' and 'only in extreme circumstances'."

"So that's what all

BUSTER
(the village stray dog)

those squiggles are."

"Don't worry, Earl. I'm going to test the formula, and I know just the person to be my guinea pig."

"Oh, you flatter me," blushed Earl. "Nobody's ever called me a nicer name than hamster in all my life."

"No, no. Not you, Earl."

Penny scratched Buster under his chin and mischievously wiggled her bottle of formula.

"I meant Housemistress Lucinda."

4

DINNERTIME AT THE ORPHANAGE

Penny stared at her plate.

Staring back at her was a gruel sandwich. The lumpy grey substance oozed out of the sides like it was trying to escape. She felt the same way, like she was sandwiched in the orphanage and wanted to ooze out of the front door and never return. She had lost her mum in a terrible car crash when she was very young. Her dad had been heartbroken. Then one day he had gone out to buy milk and never returned. She was also the only orphan in Sandwich. And that wasn't even the worse part.

Housemistress Lucinda, the orphanage housemistress, was far worse.

She sat at the other end of the dinner table. Black was

her favourite colour. Silence was her favourite song. The dictionary was her favourite book. And for reasons unknown to Penny, gruel was her favourite food. Just by looking at her, you could tell she enjoyed whacking children on the shins with her walking stick to pass the time.

When the richest man in the south of England had died without an heir, he had requested in his will that his home become what it was today. The orphanage was a huge mansion, a bit like Buckingham Palace but nicer. It had hundreds of rooms and lots of shiny stuff, and big paintings on the walls of people who never smiled. Penny knew all too well that a big house and pretty things did not make you happy.

"'Crucian,'" said Housemistress Lucinda, engrossed in her favourite book. "'A European cyprinid fish with a dark green back, a golden-yellow undersurface and reddish dorsal and tail fins.'"

She had been reading the dictionary to Penny for as long as she could remember. They were 3,831 words in, and they were still on the letter c. Penny didn't mind, because she wasn't listening. Instead, she was slowly crawling under the dining-room table.

"'Cruciverbalist,'" said Housemistress Lucinda. "'A person who enjoys or is skilled at solving crosswords.'"

Penny was very good at crawling. She didn't even make a sound as she reached Housemistress Lucinda's feet and unscrewed the bottle cap of the formula. Her cruel housemistress hated rats (because they lived in her orphanage and refused to pay any rent). It was time to create a distraction.

"'Cruddy. An American slang word for someone or something dirty, unpleasant or of poor character and quality.'" She paused. "Hmm, that must be one of those awful words unsavoury children use. You will forget that word immediately, or I will chop off your tongue and use it as a bookmark – oh good heavens, what was that?"

Penny had rolled the bottle cap across the floor, and it rattled all the way to the hallway. Housemistress Lucinda instinctively grabbed her walking stick, scuttled around the kitchen and whacked everywhere and everything in every possible direction. Meanwhile, Penny hooked her arm around the table, emptied the entire bottle into her bowl of gruel, gave it a good stir and leaped back into her chair.

"Darn rats. Think they can outsmart me."

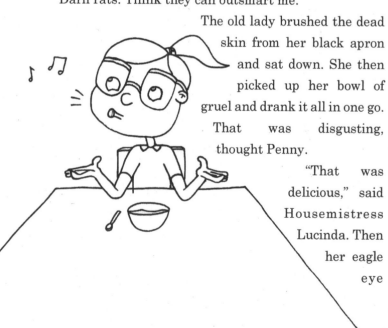

The old lady brushed the dead skin from her black apron and sat down. She then picked up her bowl of gruel and drank it all in one go. That was disgusting, thought Penny.

"That was delicious," said Housemistress Lucinda. Then her eagle eye noticed something. Her head turned towards Penny, and her nostrils growled with delight, and somehow defying the laws of nature and physics, her eyebrows pointed directly at her. "You've done something naughty."

"What? No, I haven't."

"Don't deny it, young lady. I saw the left side of your mouth curl upward. That means you have been mischievous."

"No, it doesn't. It was just a little itch."

"Don't tell me what it means," snapped Housemistress Lucinda. "I am the adult, and therefore, I am always right." She glared directly into Penny's eyes to see the truth. Annoyingly, she was very talented at it. "You've been outside again, haven't you?"

"No," lied Penny.

"Didn't you hear what I just said? I am always right, and therefore, that means you are lying. You know the rules: going outside is forbidden. This village and its citizens do not want to see an unruly child wondering the streets alone with no parents to control them. You must be punished immediately."

"But I haven't even done anything wrong. You can't punish someone for doing nothing."

"Yes, I can," said Housemistress Lucinda as she grabbed her by the wrist and dragged her out of the dining room. "This is the only way naughty children will learn. Punishment is the medicine, and segregation is the cure. You will get one day for your misbehaviour and another day for answering back."

And with that, Housemistress Lucinda threw Penny down into the cellar and locked the door.

5

SUNDAY MORNING

It was early Sunday morning.

Penny estimated she had managed to get minus two hours' sleep in the cold, damp cellar. If she had looked in the mirror, she would have discovered she had bags under her eyes. Bag-for-life bags. But there was no time for sleep. Penny checked she could hear her housemistress's snoring. She then picked the lock, silently hopped out of the window, slid down the drainpipe and ventured into Sandwich.

Maybe I'm wrong, she said to herself. I don't see any sick people. I don't hear any agonising screams. I don't smell any midnight accidents. The formula must have been safe and sound after all.

She reached the village square. It was a quiet and peaceful morning. Then she heard the sound of clip-clopping

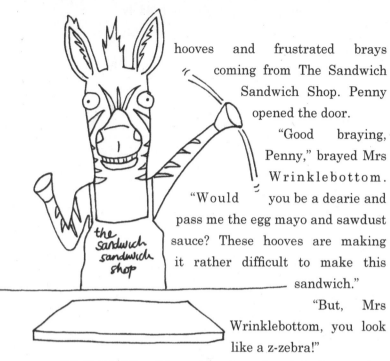

hooves and frustrated brays coming from The Sandwich Sandwich Shop. Penny opened the door.

"Good braying, Penny," brayed Mrs Wrinklebottom. "Would you be a dearie and pass me the egg mayo and sawdust sauce? These hooves are making it rather difficult to make this sandwich."

"But, Mrs Wrinklebottom, you look like a z-zebra!"

"Well, Mr Fitz did say his formula might have a few side effects." The shop owner had black and white stripes from head to toe. She had hooves where her hands used to be. When she licked her lips, her long and lumpy zebra tongue also licked her zebra nose and her zebra eyelashes too.

Penny leaned on the door frame for support. "This is terrible."

"I couldn't disagree more. I've never felt better in my whole life. My back pain, tiredness and headaches have completely disappeared thanks to Mr Fitz's Fabulous Formula. Plus I rather like my new hairstyle," she said as she brushed her black and white Mohican bristles with her hoof.

Penny sped off. She quickly reached Sandwich Church,

and the door was already open for the Sunday morning service. A very high-pitched, squeaky voice echoed from within. She prepared herself for the worst and walked inside.

"Let us give praise to our heavenly Father for the miraculous formula," squeaked Reverend Nightingale, who was ten centimetres tall and standing on her Bible.

"I was blind," oinked a villager. "But now I can see." Betty, the village butcher, was facing the wrong way, so, clearly, she still needed to wear her glasses. However, this meant that Penny caught sight of the pink and curly tail of a pig sticking out of her cardigan.

"I was lost," baaed another villager. "But now I am found." Derek, the village baker, had curly horns on the side of his head and had clearly been munching on a hymnbook.

"I was a right grumpy old git," roared Mr Dickens. "But now I can't stop smiling." The village dentist had the most wonderful set of gnashers and furry yellow mane she had ever seen. Every time he laughed and flashed those sharp-looking canine teeth, all

the other villagers
nervously shuffled
in the other
direction.

"Isn't it wonderful?"
squeaked the vicar, who was
now a little mouse. "We
have all been cured of our
ailments
and are
free to
live long and happy lives! Praise
the Lord! Now, does anyone in the congregation
know how long mice live for?"

"That depends on the company they keep," smiled Mr
Dickens.

Penny had seen and heard enough. She sped off again,
knowing exactly where she wanted to go next. The familiar
feet of a friend came into view. She was relieved to see
there were no hooves or tails or animal horns sticking out
of the cardboard box. Thankfully, no one in Sandwich had
bothered to share the formula with its lowest citizen, the
only one who couldn't afford to buy it.

"Earl, Earl, wake up. WAKE UP!"

The cardboard box rolled over. "Jumping jelly beans,"
said Earl as he stumbled to his feet. Not many people
could stand on their ceiling and sound so chirpy, but Earl
certainly could. He stepped out of what he called the "front
hole" of his cardboard box and hobbled over to Penny.

THE FORMULA!

cried Penny (with a really big exclamation mark at the end . . . like this !) "It's turning everyone into animals. Mrs Wrinklebottom looks like a zebra. Reverend Nightingale is the size of a church mouse. And Mr Dickens, who looks like a lion, is looking at everyone and licking his big, sharp teeth."

"Wax me neck, shoulders and back, and call me a surfboard!"

"I know, this is really bad. I thought it would cause side effects, but I never imagined growing a tail would be one of them."

Suddenly a hairy tail poked its way into Earl's bedroom.

"And which of the village people are you?" questioned Earl. "The village policeman? The village cowboy or maybe the village Indian? No, wait, don't tell me. I can smell cement, so you must be the village builder."

"Don't be silly, Earl. It's Buster." The dog barked to confirm his identity, then stood outside, guarding the door. He was clearly spooked by all the village creatures roaming the cobbled streets.

Earl breathed a sigh of relief and said, "What about that hairy-fingered, beardy-bottomed, stricter-than-Simon-Cowell toilet monster who has a heart as black as burnt toast?"

"You mean Housemistress Lucinda?"

29

"Yep."

"I don't know. Let's find out together."

"Excellent! My rotten leg is feeling particularly rotten this morning, so let's take my transportation device for a spin."

Earl, Penny and Buster all leaped into Earl's transportation device. He did not like calling it a shopping trolley with more than one wobbly wheel, because he was not a bag of groceries. He was a human being. He might have what looked like broccoli growing out of his ears, but he was definitely still a human.

They arrived at the orphanage. It was the most impressive house in all of Sandwich. Somebody extremely important must have lived there in the past. Penny hated the place. All those bedrooms and bathrooms and hallways and archways and reception halls and grand staircases and fountains and chandeliers . . . but no family to fill them. Housemistress Lucinda did not count.

Penny helped Earl out of his wobbly transportation device. They crept through the gardens and towards the housemistress's bedroom. Earl crouched down a little, and Penny stood on her tiptoes.

"I can see fuzzy brown fur," whispered Penny.

"I can see bigger paws and even bigger claws," replied Earl in a hushed voice. Buster growled, then whined and looked up at Penny. He must have been able to smell the animal inside, and was scared.

The duvet moved to reveal what was underneath. She was sucking her paw, dreaming of fresh salmon, and had the worst bedhead Penny had ever seen. Hibernation is no respecter of fashionable hairdos.

"Bless me socks and call me the angel Gabriel! Your snooty, head-up-her-own-backside housemistress is now a grizzly bear."

6

MR FITZ

Penny opened her eyes.

She did not know how long she had been asleep. Her eyes were so blurry and clogged up with eye gunk, she could not have told you where she was. She stretched and put her arm through the wall.

"Don't you worry about that," said a familiar voice. "I've been meaning to install a window there for some time."

"I'm sorry, Earl," she replied, carefully pulling her arm back inside. "Won't it get a bit chilly in the winter?"

"No more than usual." Earl winked with a cheeky grin on his grubby face.

The inside of Earl's cardboard box was surprisingly spacious. Penny noticed an odd smell. Then something dripped onto her shoulder. She then spotted something rectangular lying in the corner. Earl anticipated the coming questions. "The smell is mud. The drip is mud. The visitors' book is an old newspaper covered in mud. Now, would ya like some breakfast?" Earl slid a bowl of mushy brown stuff in front of Penny. She did not need him to explain what was in the bowl.

"Erm, no, thanks. I'm not hungry."

"Suit yourself. More for me and Buster." The homeless duo began to lick their breakfast until the bowl was spotless.

Penny positioned herself in front of the window she had just installed and looked outside. Suddenly the ground began to shake. What she saw next made her insides do a backward somersault. She saw a church mouse being chased by a cat, which was being chased by a hyena, which was being chased by a zebra, which was being chased by a lion, which was being chased by a hippopotamus.

"It's a safari park out there!"

"I know. Earlier this morning, while you were asleep, I ventured out. Mr Dickens tried to nibble my rotten leg. Fortunately, he didn't like it very much and spat it out." Earl rubbed his leg and whimpered. "I preferred ye olde Sandwich – you know, the boring one where nothing ever happened and nobody tried to eat each other."

"We've got to do something," said Penny. "We've got to find Mr Fitz. He must have something in his suitcase that will turn everyone back to normal."

Penny wrote a comment in Earl's visitors' book before they left: "A peaceful night's sleep and wonderful company.

33

Would suggest adding some variety to the breakfast options." Buster wanted to join them, but Penny persuaded him to stay and protect the cardboard box. He complained at first but obeyed her. Penny and Earl waited for the streets to clear of village creatures, then jumped in the shopping trolley and pelted out of town. They soon reached the neighbouring village, called Ham.

Yes, that's right . . . Ham.

They stopped outside The Blazing Donkey. (Again, I am not making this up. You should ask your parents if you can go stay at The Blazing Donkey in the village of Ham, near the town of Sandwich, for your next family holiday.) The whole area stank of beer and cigars and regrets and wasted potential, and was in desperate need of a good Febreze-ing. It was the kind of place that would be

dramatically improved by a bulldozer.

"Now listen here, Miss Penny," said

HAM

the Blazing Donkey

Earl in a protective way. "This is a job for a fully grown human, like me. They know and respect me in these kinds of dirty places. You stand behind me, okay?"

Penny nodded in agreement, and together they walked in.

"Earl, look over there," whispered Penny as she poked his good leg. "In the corner. I think that's him."

The man in the corner shimmered purple. He had attracted a small crowd with his slippery words and his suitcase filled with wonders. As they approached, his happy customers left with bottles in their hands and nothing much left in their pockets.

"I'm not taking any more appointments today. I'm needed back at Dover Hospital to perform emergency heart surgery."

"But I thought you were a travelling salesman," said Penny.

The man loosened his bow tie and mumbled, "Well, you know, I only do that on the weekends. I've got quite a few part-time jobs, depending on who you talk to."

The slippery man knew when he was about to be rumbled. He grabbed his suitcase and took off, but Earl managed to grab his collar and threw him back in his chair.

"You ain't going nowhere, Mr Fitz, unless you want me to boot you in the dangly bits."

The con man nervously glanced at Earl's leg. He never missed an opportunity – it was his thing. "With that thing? It looks as rotten as a sunken pirate ship. Is it painful?"

"Extremely painful, but I'm sure it'll manage a good kicking."

"You need my Mr Fitz's Miraculous Leg Wax. If this stuff had been around in the days of the pirates, none of 'em would have been walking around with a peg for a leg. Just rub in the wax three times a day for one week, and you'll be able to kick me all the way to Cornwall and back."

"Well, pick me nose and call me a bogey tree! I'll take three tubs."

"Earl, snap out of it! And you," said Penny as she pointed her angry finger at Mr Fitz, "my friend doesn't have any money you can cheat out of him, so quit the act and tell me what you've done to my village."

He slouched in his chair a little. "I cured them, hopefully."

"No, you didn't. You turned them into animals!"

"Really? Well, that is unfortunate," he said, scratching his head. "I'm usually at least one hundred miles away before this sort of stuff happens. You're much cleverer than all these other country folk, little girl, so I'm gonna give you a discount."

"Discount?"

"Yeah. I'll give you the antidote for half price. One thousand pounds. Now that's a bargain."

"I've got two pennies and a button," replied Penny.

"Seven hundred and fifty big ones, and that's my final offer."

"But we don't have any money at all."

"Okay, okay. We'll call it five hundred pounds, and you'll promise to never tell a soul you've robbed me blind."

"Honestly. Check our pockets if you must."

"Then I'm afraid I can't help you. Now if you'll excuse me, I really must be going. The hospital don't like to be kept waiting, and I do need to pick up my dry cleaning . . ."

Earl had heard enough. His face was redder than a sunburnt lobster. He swung his rotten leg like an enraged lumberjack. The chair that Mr Fitz was sitting on flipped upside down, and the table that Mr Fitz's suitcase was resting on snapped clean in two. The purple trickster landed on his head, and his suitcase clattered to the ground and spilled its not-so-wondrous contents everywhere.

"What's going on here, then?" shouted the barman.

"This man is extorting us," protested Penny. "He has poisoned the villagers of Sandwich and wants us to pay him for the cure."

The large barman looked at Mr Fitz, who was rubbing his head while frantically collecting all his wares. "You mean Mr Fitz the holy priest from Canterbury Monastery? Why, just last week he visited my poorly kitty-cat. He splashed holy water and said his prayers, and now Nibbles is in cat heaven. He's a saint."

"Bless you, my child." Mr Fitz smirked.

Before they could say another word, the barman grabbed them by the scruffs of their necks and threw them out of his pub.

"Well, I think that went rather well."

"How so?" complained Penny while brushing the dirt off her clothes. "We have been thrown out, and the salesman, or doctor or priest, is demanding we pay for a cure that probably doesn't even exist."

Earl dangled something shiny in front of Penny's nose. "'Cause I managed to nab us a bottle of the formula."

7

TASTE OF
HIS OWN MEDICINE

Penny twiddled her thumbs and swung her legs.
"Come on. What is taking so long?"

"Shall we play that game you taught me again?"
suggested Earl. "I'll go first. I spy with my bloodshot eye
summin' beginning with—"

"It's dirt . . . again."

"Point me north and call me a compass! You're too good
for me."

"Let's just run over the plan one more time, shall we?"

The scheming pair had decided to give Mr Fitz a taste of
his own medicine. Around two hours ago, Penny had crept
into The Blazing Donkey and poured the whole bottle of
Mr Fitz's Fabulous Formula into the con man's pint glass.

Once he turned into some sort of creepy-crawly, they would swoop in, snatch the suitcase and strike a deal – tell them where the antidote was or be a stinky animal for the rest of his miserable life. Penny was quite sure it was the best plan ever.

"Do you think he noticed?" asked Earl.

"Not one drop. He was too busy trying to sell his rubbish to the locals. All we have to do is wait a little longer."

"What d'ya reckon he'll turn into?"

Penny took a moment to think. "A sardine, because he's all slippery and shiny to look at but leaves a horrible taste in your mouth."

"Ha ha. Or maybe that silly-looking, googly-eyed, multicoloured lizard that'll trick you into thinking he's something else."

"Do you mean a chameleon?"

"That's the one. Or maybe one them little fluff balls that did a wee on my good leg last week. I wanted to kick that thing too!"

"Do you mean a rat?"

"Nope."

"A fox?"

"Nope."

"A dog?"

"Yep. That one that comes from the land of puddings and gravy and tea bags and northern nimrods."

"Do you mean a Yorkshire terrier?"

"That's the one," growled Earl. He was very protective of his legs, even the rotten one.

Suddenly a column of fire roared out from The Blazing Donkey. It felt like opening a million oven doors all at once. When the fire blast stopped, they noticed a pile of ashes where the pub sign used to be. Fully grown men screamed and ran out of the front door as though they had just seen a ghost (probably one of those really scary ones, or worse, the taxman of tax years past).

"Can sardines, chameleons or Yorkshire terriers breathe fire?" asked Earl.

Penny did not reply. She grabbed Earl by the elbow and dragged him to safety as The Blazing Donkey crumbled to the ground. Plumes of smoke swallowed the sky. Everything was on fire, even the cold-water tap. A large silhouette the size and shape of a hot-air balloon appeared in the smoke clouds.

"Pardon me, everyone. That was a nasty burp."

As the dust settled, Penny and Earl looked upward. They found themselves staring at a dragon. It was half beast, half monster and another half nightmare. It was bigger than a T. Rex, longer than an aeroplane and heavier than the moon. Its teeth were as sharp as swords, and its horns

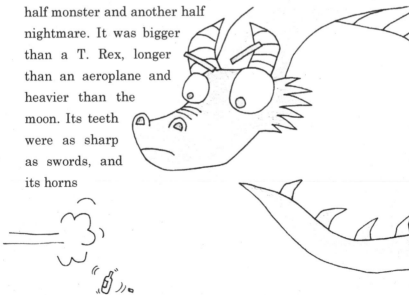

were . . . well, they were fairly normal-looking, you know, for a fearsome beast.

"What do we have here?" said the dragon. "Two scheming little weasels."

"It's okay, Penny," said Earl under his breath. "Dragons are short-sighted. Pretend to be a tree."

The dragon looked at Penny. "You're the clever girl who figured out my con."

"Oh, fiddlesticks. Maybe it is really bad at smelling stuff. Quick, think like an air freshener."

The dragon sniffed, then looked at Earl. "And you're the smelly man who kicked me in the shins."

"Oh, sugar butties. That must mean dragons can't hear nothing."

"It's not 'dragons can't hear nothing', it's 'dragons cannot hear anything'," said the dragon with perfect vision, hearing and smell. "You really must work on your vocabulary."

"So dragons have no weaknesses?" asked Penny hopefully. "Not even a little one?"

"Nope. I feel positively invincible," said Mr Fitz the dragon as he folded his tiny red arms smugly. "You two thought you could outsmart the smartest con man in England. Well, it seems that your plan has backfired. What was it you asked me to do earlier? Oh yes, give you the antidote to cure the people of Sandwich. I've got a better idea. I think I'll enslave them instead."

And with that said, Mr Fitz stretched out his brand-new wings and took off in the direction of Sandwich, leaving Penny and Earl covered in dust and despair.

8

TWENTY
LASAGNES A DAY

Eight chapters into this book, and there were now lots and lots of things happening in Sandwich, and none of it was good.

The village of Sandwich was aglow with fire and frenzy. From a distance, it looked like the villagers were celebrating bonfire night early this year. But on closer inspection, there were no sparklers or toffee apples or fireworks (however, there was a hedgehog called Bruce, the village doctor, who was very upset about his home being set on fire).

The people of Sandwich were struggling to put the fires out. That was because hippos and ostriches and aardvarks do not make very good firemen. An elephant or two would have been very useful, but fate is a cruel housemistress.

It turns out being ruled by a giant fire-breathing lizard is not the end of the world. Mr Fitz considered himself to be a very reasonable dragon overlord. Here is his list of what he expected from his village creatures:

1. Never EVER leave.
2. Do not eat each other.
3. Wee and poo wherever you like (you are animals now, so you can get away with it).
4. Make me twenty lasagnes every day.
5. Pay your taxes on time. Otherwise, you will be burned alive.
6. And finally . . .

NEVER LEAVE THE VILLAGE!

It was Penny and Earl's job to make the lasagnes. At first Mrs Wrinklebottom volunteered, but Mr Fitz preferred his food without any zebra hairs. It was tiresome, monotonous work, but it did give them time to think of a new plan. One morning, they got up extra early and laid out forty-one dishes. It was going to be a long day.

"My eyes! My eyes!" cried Earl as he continued to chop the forty-one onions. "My eyes are dribbling down my cheeks."

"You can do it," said Penny encouragingly. "We've got to prepare and cook enough for two days before we sneak out of town later." She was stirring two bubbling saucepans

with her hands while setting several timers to go off at different times with her toes. Buster was even doing his best to help by not licking any of the ingredients, even though he was hungry.

It took them all day, but they finally prepared all forty-one lasagnes. Once they had decided which looked the tastiest, Penny opened a jar of sleeping pills and emptied the entire bottle on top. After sprinkling on plenty of grated cheese, she popped the dish in the oven and turned to her partner in crime. "Right, then, let's go and read the plan one last time."

Penny and Earl took off their tomato-stained aprons, left the kitchen and walked through the orphanage's many rooms towards the library. Buster happily trotted behind them.

"I know I say this often, but your home is more magnificent than a millionaire's mansion."

"Yeah. I suppose it is quite amazing. There are loads of rooms and fancy stuff, and I don't know anyone else who has a library in their home, but there has always been something missing, you know?"

"Yeah. You need a bowling alley?"

"No. I mean a family." Buster rubbed his nose against her leg to comfort her. She rubbed under his ears in gratitude.

"Have I ever told you about my family?" said Earl as he dragged his rotten leg behind him.

"No, I don't think you have."

"Well, I come from a long line of proud non-homeowners. My dad was homeless, and his dad was homeless, and his granny was homeless, and so was her cat. It is in my guts and blood and small squishy thing between my ears."

"Where are they all now?"

"I don't know. Got nowhere to send my letters."

They turned a corner and slowed down as they passed Housemistress Lucinda's bedroom. She was still curled up in a big grizzly ball and happily hibernating. They continued to chat about families, and it made Penny wonder what her parents would have turned into if they had been alive when Mr Fitz had come to town.

They finally reached the library. Stepping inside was like walking into a cathedral. The ceiling was so high birds would nest on the top bookshelf. Penny had almost read every single book. She climbed a ladder and reached for a familiar one.

"Here it is," said Penny. "Are you sure this book is historically accurate?"

"Oh yes, I'm sure. Whack me head with a mallet and

call me a tent peg if I'm wrong!"

And so they sat down together, and Penny read The Tale of George and the Dragon to Earl and Buster one last time.

9

HAPPY
DICTATOR DAY

"**E**nter," boomed a deep voice that sounded like a gravestone falling over.

In came Penny and Earl, balancing twenty lasagnes as they walked down the aisle. They laid down their offering to the scaly tyrant, who was hanging upside down in the bell tower of the church. It was the only place a dragon could get comfortable. So the dragon had seized Sandwich Church and renamed it the Palace of Your Gracious and Merciful Dragon Overlord.

"The orphan and the bum, welcome to my palace." The dragon licked his lips with his knobbly purple tongue. "I was considering having a light snack, but now that you've arrived, I won't bother."

Reverend Nightingale breathed a sigh of relief and continued to fan her dragon overlord with a fan made from page three hundred and sixty-nine of the church hymnbook.

"Did you use tomatoes from the region of Verona, watered by Franciscan monks and nurtured by the Italian sun, as I asked?"

"Yes, Your Majesty."

"And did you go hunting for the perfect white truffle – the most expensive truffle in the world – and grate it into all the béchamel sauce, as I asked?"

"Yes, Your Majesty."

"And did you add cut-up hot dogs too?"

"Just like your mum used to, Your Majesty."

The dragon's green eyes glinted with happiness. "Splendid. You may leave," he said as he crawled down from the bell tower and began devouring his subjects' daily offering.

"Quickly, light the candles," whispered Penny.

"Okay," replied Earl. "After three. Twelve . . . thirty-seven . . . sixty-one . . . three."

Penny and Earl blew their party horns as loudly as they could, pulled their party poppers towards the dragon and sang at the top of their lungs.

HAPPY DICTATOR DAY TO YOU!
HAPPY DICTATOR DAY TO YOU!
HAPPY DICTATOR DAY DEAR YOUR
MAJESTY

HAPPY DICTATOR DAY TO YOU!

"What? What's going on?" questioned the dragon.

"Today marks exactly one month since you burned down our village and enslaved us all. We thought it would be nice to celebrate you and all the burning and tyranny and general suffering you've brought to this village," explained Penny as Buster dragged in an extra-big lasagne with birthday candles.

"Oh, how very thoughtful of you." The dragon blushed. "I knew there was a reason not to turn your pathetic little dog into ash."

"Three cheers for Mr Fitz!" roared Mr Dickens. "Hip hip hoora—!"

SILENCE!

bellowed the dragon. Everyone froze with fear as a blast of fire filled the church. Mr Dickens danced around the church, trying to put out his lion tail. "Now, why did you have to go and ruin my Dictator Day by calling me that name? As my loyal subjects, you should call me Your Majesty or Your Worshipfulness or Gracious and Merciful Dragon Overlord. From now on, anyone who calls me by my old name will be burned alive."

The dragon looked back towards Penny and smiled. "Now, where were we? Oh yes. You really shouldn't have, you lovely little girl. It means a lot to know my loyal subjects appreciate all the hard work and effort that goes into being a ruthless dictator. Thank you."

"You're welcome," replied Penny with as much fake admiration as she could muster.

Then the dragon took his cake, blew out the candles (which then relit the candles because, you know, he was a dragon), shrugged his shoulders and swallowed the whole thing in one go. "Delicious."

Penny and Earl watched intently. They immediately noticed his eyelids becoming heavier and heavier. His serpent tail slumped to the ground as the dragon yawned the biggest yawn you have ever seen, curled up and fell into a heavy sleep.

"Thank goodness for that," said Earl as he hobbled up to the dragon and kicked him in the nose with his rotten leg. He was in a deep, deep sleep and didn't even flinch. "Been wanting to do that for ages."

Everyone cheered. Mrs Wrinklebottom galloped with

glee around the church. Mr Dickens roared with delight. Reverend Nightingale bellyflopped with joy from the pulpit onto the dragon and continued to bounce up and down. Buster did a wee on his tail.

"Don't celebrate yet," said Penny. "That was just stage one."

Everyone gathered around her, as she was the clever one with the master plan. "Next is stage two," she said as she held up the picture book called The Tale of George and the Dragon. "Then comes stage three," she said as she flicked to the last few pages and presented everyone with a double page spread of a gallant knight plunging his sword into the dragon's heart. "Then finally comes stage four," she said as she turned the page to reveal a dead dragon and a cheering crowd of people.

"You can do it, Penny," squeaked the Reverend.

"We all believe in you, but we're not so sure about him," growled Mr Dickens as he pointed a claw at Earl.

"Can he really be trusted with something so important?" said Mrs Wrinklebottom as she nervously rubbed her hooves together.

Earl shrugged his shoulders. He was used to everybody telling him that he was good for nothing. Buster wagged his tail and barked loudly in favour of her plan. Penny decided to ignore the villagers' comments. There was not a single moment to lose, not even in defending her friend. They rushed out of the church, leaped into Earl's transportation device, and off they zoomed on their important quest to find themselves a George.

10

BEWARE
HERE BE KNIGHTS

The pictures in the storybook depicted a brave knight.

George wore shiny armour from head to toe and carried a sword twice as long as his arm. He rode into battle on a white horse and had a red cloak that wafted behind him heroically. Penny decided the golden halo was optional, but the rest was essential.

Penny and Earl had lost count of how many towns and villages they had visited. They had been searching all night and all day, and still they had not found him. They had managed to find some people called George, but none of them really looked like a dragon slayer. Here's a quick recap:

- George the Cabbage Farmer from Richborough, who had never held a sword or worn steel armour in his life.
- George the Public Toilet Enthusiast, who was travelling the length and breadth of Great Britain to visit (and use) all the public toilets and document his porcelain adventures.
- George the Fishmonger from Cliffsend Market, who did sell swordfish but, when asked if he would fight a dragon, replied, "Not for all the fish in the ocean."
- George the Village Idiot of Ramsgate, who had the courage and charm of a soggy dishcloth.
- George the Sausage Dog from Sandwich Bay, who was too preoccupied with chasing his tail to slay a dragon.

As you can see, none of them matched the George – a valiant knight who could single-handedly fight and defeat a dragon – from the storybook.

"This is hopeless," said Earl as he collapsed on the side of the road from exhaustion. "We're never going to find him."

"Don't say that," said Penny.

"But we have almost run out of time," said Earl, trying to hold back a yawn. "The greedy dragon will be waking up soon and expecting his brekkie."

"It's been taken care of, remember? Mrs Wrinklebottom is going to cover for us. We can't let everyone down. We must carry on. We've got to find us a knight called George."

Earl glanced to the side of the road and noticed a wooded area. To you and me, it would look like a mess of trees and mud and leaves and twigs. However, Earl saw cosy hammocks swinging from trees and relaxing mud bubble baths and snuggly pillows made of leaves and comfy mattresses made of twigs.

"How about we change our tactics? Instead of being a hot dog, we become a sausage and a bun."

"You mean split up?"

"Exactly. That way, we'll be able to do twice the amount of George-searching. You go on to the next town ahead, and I'll take a look in these here woods."

"Really? What would a knight be doing in the woods?"

"Erm," ermed Earl. "Could be doing some knight training, or going for a wee."

Penny nodded in agreement. "Good point. Let's meet back here in three hours, and hopefully, one of us will have found our guy. Remember, everyone in Sandwich thinks you're good for nothing, but I know you can do good for the village. Time to prove them all wrong, Earl. Good luck." She waved goodbye and walked off towards the next village.

Earl jumped for joy. He was as giddy as a drunk cloud. As he hobbled into the woods, he was so overcome with whimsiness that he completely missed the warning sign. It would not have mattered, because he couldn't read, but you can read, so you might as well have a look.

And that wasn't the only one he missed as he hobbled around the woods, trying to find the perfect spot for a peaceful kip. He also missed this one.

And he missed this one too.

Earl was about to lower his rotten leg down beside a comfortable-looking patch of grass when a sudden cry threw him off balance.

"Halt! Who goes there?" demanded a high-pitched voice.

Earl toppled over and landed in a puddle. "Who said that?" he spluttered. He looked around and saw nobody.

"Well, I asked first," replied the mystery voice.

"I'm just a lowly peasant from Sandwich."

"Liar! I can smell the onions on your breath. You are a French spy, come to poison our fertile English lands and sow discord in the hearts and minds of the people against the crown."

"No, no," pleaded Earl. "You're mistaken. I have been enslaved and forced to chop onions to make twenty lasagnes a day."

"Even worse, he's Italian," said the voice, which Earl was beginning to think was coming from a nearby tree. "Before we send you back to your maker, allow us to introduce ourselves. My name is Ge, and this is Or, Gi and Na, my brave and chivalrous companions."

"Hello," said Or.

"Nice to meet you," said Gi.

"The pleasure is ours," said Na.

"We are the Four Horseradishes of the Apostrophe," said Ge.

ATTACK!

11

WHATS A HORSERADISH?

"Prepare to die, scum."

What Earl had not noticed earlier were the four hairy vegetables poking out of the ground. They leaped out of the earth, carrying tiny swords and shields made of twigs. The horseradish is an extremely underestimated vegetable, as you are about to find out.

"Charge!" shouted Ge, who was clearly the leader.

Earl, being a lowly peasant, had become very good at dodging strange-looking vegetables. He picked up his rotten leg and hopped as fast as he could, which was pretty fast indeed. He looked behind him to check on his fearsome attackers and noticed they were already one hundred metres behind.

"Do not bother to beg for mercy, pig!" yelled Or as the horseradishes slowly inched closer.

"Erm, okay, then," replied Earl.

"He's very fast," said Gi, panting for breath. "It would be easier if he stood still and let us catch him up. Do you think we could ask politely?"

"No, brothers and sisters. We are brave knights charging the enemy. Steel yourself and prepare for victory!" shouted Ge. They began to run faster, which was about as fast as a misshapen cabbage rolling uphill.

"I'm getting tired," said Na. "Can we have a short rest?"

They stopped running for a quick breather.

"Excuse me," shouted Earl, who was now two hundred metres ahead. "Did I hear you say that you are knights?"

"Yes," replied Ge proudly. "We are the Four Horseradishes of the Apostrophe, Knights of the Woodlands, protectors of the realm, and we must conquer the invaders and pillagers and enemies of our beloved woods."

"And how were you going to do that?" asked Earl.

"Well, if you let us catch you up, we'll poke you really hard in the shins until – SNAP! – you

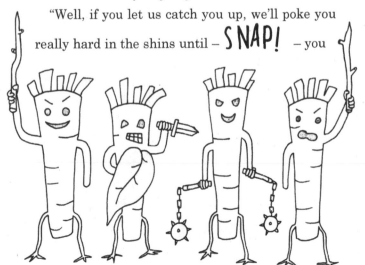

break into millions of tiny pieces."

"Oh," replied Earl, who was clearly impressed. It is important to mention that Earl had never actually met a knight before. Penny had read *The Tale of George and the Dragon* to him quite a few times, and he had enjoyed all the pictures, but Earl was the sort of person who would believe anything. So if he met four talking horseradishes who called themselves knights, then that was exactly what they were.

"Excuse my intrusion," said Earl as he hobbled towards them and bowed before the vegetables, "good Knights of the Woodlands. I mean you and your realm no harm."

"I like this one," said Or. "Polite, and a fast runner too. He would make a fine stallion."

"Pardon me saying this, sires and siresses, but you look a little different from the pictures in the book."

He held out the book and flicked through the pages. The horseradishes looked at each other and laughed.

"We are not like those namby-pamby human knights," explained Gi, "who wear polished armour to hide their wimpy muscles and prance about on horseback like sissies. We are vegetable knights. We are at one with the earth. We protect this sacred woodland. We listen to the leaves and look after the twigs and fight off beasties who think they can go wee-wee on our trees."

"And what if there was –" Earl paused to find the right word "– a gigantic fire-breathing dragon in the vicinity?"

The Four Horseradishes of the Apostrophe huddled together for a team talk. Earl heard the words "dangerous" and "singed eyebrows" and "a knight's sworn duty" more than once. Enough time passed for the peasant to wonder if Penny was having as much luck as him. Eventually, they broke off the private discussion.

"Excuse me, peasant man."

"Yes, Sir Vegetable. The name's Earl."

"Earl," replied Ge with a concerned look on his face. "What does this dragon you speak of eat?"

"Twenty lasagnes."

The vegetable knights recoiled and gasped.

"A day."

Na toppled over in shock.

"And they're full of all sorts of vegetables."

"My fellow knights, it is just as we feared. The dragon is a *vegetarian*. Tell me," said Ge as he turned to Earl, "do any of these lasagnes contain mushrooms?"

"Oh, yes, wild ones. Me and Penny have to pick one hundred each morning."

"Heavens above! And what about garlic?"

"Oh, yes, many innocent wild garlics are plucked 'n' chopped 'n' boiled alive. I am surprised we don't smell the lizard's breath from here."

"Goodness gracious! I dare not mention the poor herbs."

"Well, we use freshly plucked basil, rosemary and thyme. He eats so much we have to walk further and further each day to forage for all the ingredients."

"Enough! We have heard enough," said Ge dramatically. "We have heard enough of this foul beast and its despicable crimes against the woodlands. We must act now. This greedy dragon cannot be allowed to live. We accept your holy quest to defeat the Dragon of Sandwich. Lead the way."

Earl smiled. He had done something useful (in his head, at least). It felt good, like a warm, fuzzy cowpat melting around his heart. "Thank you, brave knights. I can't wait to tell Penny the good news."

12

NOBLE STEEDS WITH KNOBBLY KNEES

"And the moment I plunged my sword into the Dragon of Suffolk's heart, I knew I wanted to be a heroic knight for the rest of my days."

Penny clapped. She had finally found him.

The knight in shining armour, who was currently sitting on a stone wall, had been weaving his heroic stories all afternoon. Penny was mesmerised by his curly blonde hair and dreamy blue eyes, as deep as the ocean's back pocket. If someone could defeat the dragon and free the people of Sandwich, it was going to be him.

"Did I mention the dragon had poisonous fangs?"

"No," said Penny. "I don't think you did."

"How could I forget those fangs? Sharper than a

Frenchman's tongue, with venom that turns your insides into gravy. One wrong move, and I'd have oozed out of the gaps in my armour."

Penny gasped.

"And did I mention the battle took place inside an active volcano?"

The second gasp sucked in a fly.

"And the sun was in my eyes."

Penny coughed, as she couldn't gasp any more. She let out all the air in her lungs, creating a sound of sheer adoration. The poor fly made a run for it.

"And I should also mention that I had cramp in my left leg."

Penny clapped in amazement and, in doing so, squished the fly. "Earl is going to be so pleased I found you." She danced on the spot in excitement, then said, "Remind me what your name is again."

"My name is Sir George the Legendary Dragon Slayer, Earl of Eastbourne, Duke of Devon, Baron of Bristol, Knight of the Round Table, Lord of the Realm, and protector of the people of England."

"Do you mind if I just introduce you as George?"

"Sir George will suffice."

Then the sound of hooves drifted down the road. Penny could see something in the distance. It was Earl, trotting down the road while knocking together two halves of a coconut. She skipped towards him, excited to share her big news. Earl neighed and then came to a halt in front of her.

"I've found him, Earl. I've found the knight," squealed Penny with joy while pointing behind her.

Earl looked down the road and saw the towering metal man shining in the afternoon sun. "Oh, fiddlesticks. But I found knights too."

"Really? I don't see your knight anywhere. Have you seen my Sir George? Did you know he once defeated a pack of ravenous wolves with nothing but a toothpick and still made it back to his castle in time for dinner?"

"Oh, really?" said Earl, puffing up his chest. "Well, my knights have defeated . . . erm . . ."

"Psst, noble steed," whispered Or, who had been sitting in Earl's pocket the entire time. "Tell her about our ferocious chasing abilities."

"Oh yes, they are particularly skilled at chasing slow-moving enemies, and they have also taught me how to be a noble steed."

"He's a natural with the coconut shells," said Na, poking out of Earl's left pocket. "You can't teach that. Believe me, we've tried."

"Who's a clever boy?" added Gi, who climbed up out of his collar and rubbed Earl's beard affectionately as if it were a horse's mane. Earl neighed. Penny was speechless.

Ge leaped off the noble steed's saddle and yelled, "Knights of the Woodlands, assemble."

Penny watched in utter bewilderment as four horseradishes jumped off her friend, rolled to the ground and began swishing and stabbing the air with their little sharpened twigs. This was the first time she had seen talking vegetables, and the first time she had been poked in the ankle by one too.

"Ouch!"

"Apologies, milady." Gi curtsied. "I got a bit carried away."

Ge gathered together his knights and shouted upward to Penny in the deepest voice possible, about the depth of a pumpkin's voice. "We have heard of your terrible plight under the vegetarian beast, fair maiden. Fear not. We are here to answer your call to arms. We, the Four Horseradishes of the Apostrophe, will gallop into the dragon's lair on our noble steed and then slay the monster."

Penny was still speechless. Earl noticed this and, having fully embraced his new role, licked her cheek and robbed a Polo from her pocket. "Isn't it great? Not one but four knights, and I've found my dream job. So, do you want to tell Sir George he can go home, or shall I do it?"

"Aaaah," said Penny, having finally remembered the first letter of the alphabet. The rest soon came flooding back. "No, no, no. This can't be right. None of them are called George."

"Oh, pardon my manners. I haven't properly introduced you." Earl bent down on his good knobbly knee and said,

"This is Ge, Or, Gi and Na. Together they are Georgina."

Penny crossed her arms and clenched her jaw and made her eyebrows quiver with rage. "No. This is ridiculous. Whoever heard of a vegetable knight or a twig sword? It's absurd. Sir George is a real knight with real armour and a real sword and real experience with fighting dragons. So you can all go back to your woodland."

"We cannot go back now," protested Or. "We are knights. We have sworn a sacred oath to protect the helpless, and we will carry out our honourable duties to the bitter end."

"And what exactly are you going to do? Challenge him to a duel?"

"Precisely," replied Ge. "Charge!"

They watched as the four heroic vegetables waved their twigs and slowly charged down the road. Earl was eager to join in and banged his coconut shells together in excitement. "That's my cue. Wish me luck."

13

GEORGE VS GEORGINA

The etiquette of a duel is very simple.

One opponent chooses the location, and the other chooses the weaponry. Then they bow, shout, "God save the King," and the rest is fairly obvious. Neither Penny nor Earl had seen a duel before. Then again, no one had ever seen a duel quite like this before.

Sir George did not carry a chopping board with him wherever he went. So when four woodland vegetables challenged him to a duel, he had to chose the next best location – a nearby field. The horseradishes decided they should play to their somewhat limited strengths and so choose their favourite weaponry – rock, paper, scissors.

"I've never heard of this fighting style before," questioned Sir George. "Is it from the Middle East?"

"Dunno," replied Or. "We'd be happy to explain the rules."

"Please don't. I hate rules. Besides, I've trained under Sir Galahad for six years in hand-to-hand combat, so I'll manage just fine."

Meanwhile, Penny was standing next to Earl at the side of the field. She wanted to move in for a closer look, but Earl insisted he should stay tied to the fence, like Sir George's horse. They watched on as the knights warmed up.

"This is going to be a very one-sided battle," commented Penny.

"Yep, I agree. Four against one is a bit unfair."

"You can't seriously believe the vegetables stand a chance against a real-life knight. Sir George is going to crush them – he might even eat them alive if he's peckish."

"Never judge a book by its cover," replied Earl as he threw an evil glare at the horse next to him. "Can you believe that guy? Thinks he's so smart with a swishy tail and hooves. I'm just as good at being a horse."

The horse lifted its tail and did a massive poo.

"Show-off."

In the middle of the field, the duel was about to start.

"First to three wins," said Ge.

"Sure," replied Sir George, who was not listening. The knight clenched his armoured fist and slung his arm back, ready to strike.

"Right, then, let's begin. Round one. Three, two, one, GO!"

Sir George unleashed his powerful bicep. The four horseradishes, in perfect synchronicity, lay on the ground side by side in perfect formation. The steel fist missed and whooshed past.

"Ha ha! That's one to us," shouted Or triumphantly. "Paper beats rock, you dim-witted buffoon."

Their opponent was not listening. He was pumped up and in the zone. He used the momentum from the first swing, spun around and took aim.

"Round two. Three, two, one—"

SLAM!

"Drat," said Or.

Years of practice meant the vegetables had very quick reaction times. They had managed to avoid the attack and were lying in the shape of a pair of scissors next to Sir George's clenched fist. "The buffoon outsmarted us. Two rocks in a row, what an ingenious move. You are a truly worthy foe."

Sir George was getting angry. You could tell, because steam began to rise from his closed helmet. He shouted a hardened battle cry and readied for his next attack.

"Final round. Thr—"

Penny and Earl cringed at what they saw next. Sir George had slammed his steel-plated foot as hard as he could into the ground. He had squashed his opponent.

"Well, I did warn you," sighed Penny. "Your little friends didn't stand a chance."

Earl did not say anything for the next five seconds. He watched as the knight began to walk back towards them with a victorious spring in his step. Then Earl said, "Tie me legs to a tree and me arms to another, and call me a lumpy hammock. Look."

Up came a horseradish, followed by three more. The ground around them was quite muddy, and when they had been stepped on, they had simply sunk into the ground while in the rock position.

"Oi, where do you think you're going?" shouted Ge. "Cheating is an ugly habit. Now come back here, and make one of the three official shapes pre-approved by the Rock, Paper, Scissors Governing Body."

By now Sir George had had enough. He drew his sword and charged. The horseradishes needed no encouragement. It was, after all, their favourite thing about being knights. They charged each other and engaged in vegetable combat. Using their lightning reflexes, they dodged the blade and leaped onto the knight's armour. Sir George tried to swat them off, but his heavy and cumbersome armour

71

prevented him, and he began to lose his balance.

The knight toppled over and landed face first in a cowpat. The horseradishes were extremely pleased but not entirely satisfied. They jumped up and down on the knight's helmet so that it sank in some more.

"Well," said Earl smugly. "I did warn you. Your shiny friend didn't stand a chance."

Sir George stumbled to his feet and took off his soiled helmet. "The reward for defeating this Dragon of Sandwich better be good. How much did you say you were paying, little girl?"

"You never asked."

"Well, I am now. How much, kid?"

"Erm, nothing."

"What!"

"We don't have any money, but you will be fulfilling your sworn duty as an honourable knight by defending those who are defenceless and freeing those who have been enslaved."

By now Sir George had managed to clean his ears and empty his helmet. She could tell he was not the slightest bit impressed, so she quickly added, "And I'll throw in twenty lasagnes too."

"Oh dear, little girl. You read too much fiction. This armour doesn't come cheap, and my noble steed needs shelter and grooming."

"He's right, you know," added Earl. "Steeding is no picnic."

The knight decided not to put his helmet back on. He

jumped onto his horse and galloped off into the distance in search of someone who had disposable income. He did not even say goodbye.

"Do not be dismayed, milady." Ge stepped forward to speak. "You are in the presence of true knights. My brethren and I know the meaning of honour and bravery and courage. We will defeat the dragon and free your village."

Earl clapped.

The vegetables bowed.

Penny sulked.

14

BACK
IN CHURCH

If you think that dads snore loudly, then you've never heard a dragon snore.

The Dragon Overlord of Sandwich was still asleep. The Dictator Day lasagne, laced with sleeping pills, had worked a treat. Every time the dragon snored, a fairy lost its hearing. With each new snore, another crack appeared in the mortar between the stones in the wall.

"My beautiful church," whimpered Reverend Nightingale. "Ruined! It's ruined!"

"There, there, it's all right. God wouldn't want you to cry, I think." Mr Dickens was not very good at consoling people, as you can tell. Buster, on the other hand, was very good at consoling people and gave the mouse a gentle lick and a thoughtful whine. Despite being a lion, Mr Dickens was still a gentleman, so he demonstrated this by handing the church mouse his tail.

"Thanks," replied the Reverend as she blew her nose on the fluffy bit.

"What's taking them so long?" questioned Mrs Wrinklebottom, who had plugged her zebra ears with the insides of those pretty little cushions you kneel on to pray. "Mr Fitz could wake up at any time."

Suddenly Mr Dickens had a eureka moment. "Fork!" roared the lion as he leaped into the air and began chasing his soggy tail with glee.

"But we've already tried a fork."

"No, we haven't."

"Yes, we have. See for yourself." Mrs Wrinklebottom pointed her hoof towards a big pile of bent and broken implements: kitchen knives, a flagpole, sharpened crucifixes, dozens of forks, even the pointy bit on the top of the church spire. They had been attempting to stab the sleeping dragon all day, but nothing was strong enough to penetrate his armoured scales.

"Hold your horses," said the lion. "We've tried normal forks, but what about a pitchfork?"

The church mouse's tiny eyes sparkled with hope. "The dentist has got a point – three actually."

"That's brilliant," agreed the zebra. "Three big, sharp, pointy bits for three times the poking power."

Buster had already gone in search of a pitchfork and returned with a good specimen clenched between his teeth.

They each
took a section of
the pitchfork, aimed for
where they thought the
dragon's heart was and
charged.

SNAP!
TWANG!
THUMP!

Having bounced around the church like pinballs, the three villagers ended up in a mangled pile at the other end of the church, rubbing their sore bottoms. The dragon, however, did not even have a scratch and simply breathed out. The snore echoed around the church like an overweight poltergeist. They continued to discuss other potential sharp objects for the next five minutes until Mrs Wrinklebottom noticed something.

"I just noticed something."

"Please don't judge me. I haven't cleaned my teeth in months."

"No, it's not that," she said as got up on her hooves. "It

seems awfully quiet, don't you think?"

The mouse crept up to their dragon overlord, as mice do oh-so well. Reverend Nightingale crawled all over the beast, inspecting every inch, and returned with a smile as big as the moon.

"We did it. We actually did it. At last our captor is dead."

"Are you sure?" questioned Mr Dickens while stroking his mane. "You'd think his tongue would be sticking out or something."

"I'm quite sure. He hasn't breathed in over five minutes."

Buster barked triumphantly.

"Huzza!" cried Mrs Wrinklebottom. "The pitchfork must have caused some delightful internal bleeding. So I didn't have to cook all those lasagnes after all. Anyone peckish?"

Suddenly a very different sound shook the church building. Several loose tiles fell off the roof, and spiders fell off their webs. That did not bother the Reverend too much, but the fact that the sound was more of a yawn than a snore did bother her. They all turned around and watched as the sleepy tyrant awoke from his slumber. Mr Fitz stretched like a dog and said, "That was a wonderful nap."

"Really? Are you sure?" questioned the mouse.

"Yes, my little loyal subject. I'd go so far as to say that was possibly the best night's sleep I've ever had."

"No sudden heart aneurysms or nightmares about sharp, pointy objects?"

"None whatsoever. Why do you ask?"

"Oh, just curious," replied the mouse innocently as the lion and the zebra hurriedly hid all the broken sharp, pointy objects.

"Your concern for my well-being is most comforting, Reverend. I shall try my best not to step on you today."

"Thank you, Your Majesty."

"Now send for Penny and the smelly one to bring me my breakfast. I'm starving."

Mrs Wrinklebottom trotted out of the church. A few seconds later, she then trotted back in, pulling a cart piled high with lasagne. Mrs Wrinklebottom was a very good cook. On the other hand, zebras are not very good at wearing oven mitts. She tried to serve the lasagne dishes, most of which slipped between her hooves and smashed on the stone floor in front of the dragon. Red sauce oozed down the aisle. Buster held in his tongue, knowing what would happen if he licked it up.

"Did you use tomatoes from the region of Verona, watered by Franciscan monks and nurtured by the Italian sun?"

"Not exactly, Your Majesty. Although the local tomatoes have been 'watered' by the village monkeys."

"And what about the Italian white truffle?"

"Had to settle for a brown one, Your Majesty."

"And the hot dogs?"

"That I did manage, Your Majesty."

"Good, so not a complete disaster, then."

"I shouldn't mention the disaster. It would spoil the surprise. And do watch out for zebra hairs. If they get stuck in your throat, you'll be coughing for days."

The dragon looked displeased. You could tell, because

the fire in his eyes burned a vibrant orange and the temperature in the church shot up. "Where are my lasagne chefs?"

The three villagers looked at each other for inspiration. Seeing as they managed to muster none, they settled for silence.

"Where is Penny?" said the dragon, now with fire in his eyes and his words.

"She is . . . errr . . . brushing her hair, Your Majesty."

Mr Fitz had heard enough. He rose up on his powerful hind legs and roared with the fury of a thousand geography teachers. The three of them instantly knew what was about to happen next, and legged it. Brilliant flames engulfed the entire building. The heat and intensity of the dragon's fire singed the heavens above. The fire even set God's fire alarm off.

I do not envy any who dare battle the beast.

Meanwhile, the sound of Mr Fitz's rage rumbled through the town. It uncobbled the cobbled streets. It unthatched the thatched roofs. It even travelled all the way to the orphanage and unhinged the hinged front door.

Being woken up early is very annoying – just ask your parents. So being woken up three months early is extremely infuriating and a crime worthy of having your face bitten off. That's why you should never disturb a grizzly bear from hibernation.

But it was too late now.

Housemistress Lucinda was awake.

15

FAIL TO PREPARE
PREPARE TO FAIL

Earl crouched down behind the stone wall surrounding the church. As he did so, he let his rotten leg stretch out like a beach towel. The horseradishes had climbed the wall and were peeking their tufts over for a look.

"Are you sure this is the right place?" questioned Or. "I thought dragons lived in underground lairs or mountain caves, not churches."

"Our noble steed must be wrong," declared Ge. "Clearly the dragon has heard the many tales of the Four Horseradishes of the Apostrophe and is in hiding. Let us split up and hunt down the terrible beast."

"Be patient, knights," replied Earl. "Just wait and see."

It was difficult to do any seeing, as there was currently nothing to see. From the outside, the church looked as it always did. Big and stony and as bland as an empty casserole dish. No one was in sight. All the villagers were hiding in their basements, trying their very best not to eat their neighbours. The knights and Earl waited patiently. Then a large gorilla wearing dark sunglasses and an earpiece tapped Earl on the shoulder.

"Excuse me. You know the rules. No loitering on the grounds of the Dragon Overlord of Sandwich. Move along, please, move along."

The four vegetables turned to face their foe. "So, at last the beast confronts its fate."

"What did you call me?"

"A beast, and you're certainly a big one," said Or. "Would you mind kneeling down when we do battle?"

"Beast? Do battle? But I'm just the bodyguard."

"Ignore the beast, men. It is trying to trick us." Ge raise his twig sword in the air and shouted at the confused gorilla. "Surrender, or prepare to be slain by the Knights of the Woodlands."

Earl stepped in. "Stop. No surrendering needed here. This ain't no dragon. It's Terrence."

The gorilla smiled at the mention of his name and waved. "Welcome to Sandwich, visitors. Sorry for all the burning buildings and rubble and animal droppings. I used to be the local blacksmith, you know, until Mr Fitz came to town. Now I'm his bodyguard." He leaned towards Earl and whispered, "Wasn't the plan to find a knight called

George?"

"Yep," said Earl. "I did even better. I got four knights. Ain't they marvellous?"

Terrence scratched his head. "You sure you two know what a knight looks like?"

"Oi, hairy carpet man," snapped Na, who was quite offended. "Being a knight has nothing to do with how big you are or how thick your armour is or how many dragons you've slain. It is a state of mind. Take us to the beast. We will defeat your evil oppressor and prove our worth."

Terrence looked at Earl.

Earl smiled.

"Speechless. We often have that effect. Do not fear, for we have a plan," declared Ge. "While the dragon slumbers, we hold the element of surprise."

Before Terrence the gorilla could make an appropriate response, a low rumbling interrupted him. The ground shuddered like a steam train hitting the emergency brakes. Ge, Or, Gi and Na all fell off the wall. Earl found the vibrations rather therapeutic for his rotten leg. Terrence was quite used to the regular earthquakes and stood his ground.

"Monkey nuts," cursed Terrence. "Time for a new plan. The dragon has awoken. Where is Penny? She'll know what to do."

"Ah," replied Earl. "Well, we may have had a teeny, tiny difference of opinion."

"What?"

"I believe her exact words were 'Only an empty-headed

fool with a cauliflower for a brain would send a horseradish to battle a dragon.'"

"Do not split any hairs, carpet man, for the Knights of the Woodlands have many skills."

"I've been meaning to ask," said Terrence. "What strengths do you have?"

"Far too many to list, hairy one."

"Is flame retardancy one of them?"

"Strange question. Why do you ask?"

The sound of hooves thundering down the church path, followed by a loud explosion and flames bursting out of the church's front door rudely interrupted them. A zebra galloped past. Earl could have sworn a lion with a burning mane was riding it, along with a dog and a mouse clinging on for dear life.

Mrs Wrinklebottom shouted as she galloped off. "He's all warmed up for you."

"Good luck," added a squeaky voice.

Terrence tried to remember the George that Penny had described from her book. That George was almost as big as the dragon and was standing triumphantly on the slain dragon without a scratch on his armour. He even had both his eyebrows. Earl had made a terrible mistake. He could not let the little vegetables go in there. He may have been turned into a gorilla, but he had a conscience, and it was telling him to, at the very least, wrap them in kitchen foil first.

"Let's not confront Mr Fitz just yet. I think we should wait until Penny gets here. Then, after a good night's sleep, we'll think of a plan and come back tomorrow fully prepared."

There was no answer.

"What do you think, Earl?"

Again he did not get an answer.

"And you, Mrs Wrinklebottom?"

Yep, you guessed it. No answer.

Mrs Wrinklebottom had common sense. She knew the best thing to do was to run in the opposite direction. Earl lacked common sense. He did, however, enjoy being a trusty steed as he trotted towards the church, carrying the four vegetable knights. And as we have already discovered, the horseradishes did not have a clue how dangerous a dragon really is.

16

THE
TRAVELLING SALES WITCH

Penny's mind was full of thoughts as she ran down the dirt road. She had a tricky dilemma. Should she:

    a) continue her search for a knight called George, only to return to the scorched remains of her friend, seasoned with burnt horseradish

    b) turn around and face the dragon with her friend and unlikely champions in the knowledge that they were doomed?

It was a tough one.

Penny was convinced that if Earl had drunk the formula,

he would have turned into a donkey, not a horse. His plan was to trot into the dragon's lair with four overconfident vegetables perched on his shoulder. She feared his plan was flawed. Maybe everyone in Sandwich was right, and he was good for nothing.

If only she could find Sir George and persuade him to fight. Maybe she could offer the knight the town's riches, she thought to herself. Of course, the town did not have any riches, but that was a dilemma for another day. Or perhaps she could promise to bestow a new title on him to add to his already lengthy name. She decided "the Savoury Saviour of Sandwich" had a nice ring to it.

Deep in thought, Penny did not notice the wooden cart ahead travelling towards her. She bumped her head on it and fell to the ground.

"Oi, watch where you're walking!" said an old lady who was pulling the wooden cart.

"Sorry. I was just, erm . . ."

"Honestly, youth of today. Too busy contemplating tricky dilemmas to look where they're going."

"How did you know that I was—?"

"Deep in contemplation over a moral dilemma? It was all over your face like yesterday's dinner. Still is. You should learn to wash your face, my dear."

"Have you by any chance seen—?"

"A knight called Sir George ride past on a horse the colour of moonlight? Nope, never heard of the fella."

"Would you please stop—?"

"Finishing your sentences? Sorry. I can't help it. Comes

with the job."

Penny brushed the dust from her bum and asked, "Who are you?"

The old lady reached into her cart and pulled out a big black pointy hat. She placed it carefully on her head and then pulled a lever. Her wooden cart suddenly and miraculously transformed into a wooden room.

Penny read the sign above the door. "'Gaze into your future with Aunt Maggie.'"

"That's me. I'm a fortune teller. The crystal ball is my only friend. It helps me see into your past, present and future."

Penny rolled her eyes, the universal sign for "Codswallop."

"Don't believe me? Give an old lady a chance to prove herself." Aunt Maggie pushed the door open and said, "Step into my world, my child, and I will help solve your dilemma."

By now Penny had run out of options. She stepped inside and sat down. It was dark and smelt of festering hopes and forgotten dreams. Then a ball of shimmering light glided down from above and — hovered between her and the fortune teller. Old, wrinkly hands gently stroked the ball until something appeared. At first it was fuzzy, but the images slowly became clearer.

She saw a dragon.

She saw Earl and the horseradishes about to die.

She saw a girl burst in, holding a potion and throwing it over the dragon.

She saw the dragon melt away.

She saw the formula wear off and all the townsfolk turn back to normal.

Then she saw nothing but a brilliant white light.

Penny was perplexed. How could a little potion defeat a dragon? Who was the girl? Could girls be knights and slay dragons? She found her voice and asked, "Would you mind rewinding your crystal ball? I'd like to watch it again."

"Rewind?" coughed the fortune teller. "What do you think this is? Some kind of entertainment service?"

"But I need to know who the girl is, the one who slew the dragon with the potion. I need to find her."

"My child, the girl is you."

"Really?" questioned Penny. "Are you sure it was me?"

The old lady inspected her shining ball. "Darn smudges," cursed Aunt Maggie. "I really must remember to clean my crystal ball before readings. Of course it was you. You are the knight."

"But how did I do it? I don't know how to make a potion that will defeat a dragon."

"The crystal ball does not show us the journey. It can only show us the end." The old lady grabbed her hand and led her back into the real world. "This is the wonderful thing about our future, my child. Impatience is the root of all life's problems, you cannot force the future to appear. Instead, you must let it unfold before you."

"What?"

"Just pull that lever, and you'll see what I mean."

17

ANYTHING
IS FOR SALE

Penny pulled a different lever, and suddenly the wooden room, which was originally a wooden cart, folded and unfolded and twisted and transformed into a wooden market stall. She walked to the front and read the sign. "*Aunt Maggie's Witch Brewery.*"

The old lady popped up inside the stall. She was still wearing the pointy hat, only now she was also wearing a stripy apron with a name badge pinned to it. "See, patience is a virtue and all that rubbish. Right, I better get to work."

Aunt Maggie then bent down and started mumbling to herself in search of strange ingredients. She said stuff like "unicorn tears" and "unshaven legs of a spider" and "three-year-old Pritt Stick". Some of it I will not repeat, as it would turn your stomach upside down and inside out.

Penny had many questions. She began with "Didn't you say you were a fortune teller?"

"I am, my dear, but I dabble in all forms of witchery. You can't rely on one stream of income these days, you know."

"Are you going to make a magic potion for me?"

"I certainly hope so, unless you fancy a spider's-leg omelette?" Aunt Maggie threw all her collected ingredients into a cauldron, waved her arms about, then muttered gibberish under her breath while stirring the mixture. Suddenly a big puff of smoke filled the stall. Penny tried her best to waft the smoke away, and as she did, she saw a bottle full of potion sitting on the counter. It glowed a deep red and was in a spray bottle, the kind hairdressers use to wet your hair (and the insides of your ears). She looked at the bottle suspiciously.

"I can see you are not convinced." Aunt Maggie rubbed her hands together and cackled loudly. Clearly, this was her favourite part of the sales pitch. "How about a little demonstration?"

The witch grabbed the bottle and walked to the side of the dirt road. She looked around and found a little grey mushroom. As she bent down, her knees creaked. Aunt Maggie pointed the spray bottle at the mushroom and looked at Penny. "Watch this."

She squished the trigger.

A cloud of red droplets covered the mushroom.

The little mushroom began to shake.

Then up from the ground sprouted a fully clothed young boy.

Penny gasped.

The boy smiled.

Aunt Maggie kicked him. "If I ever see your grubby little hands near my wares again, I'll make mushroom soup of you. Now get outta here."

The boy nodded apologetically and ran as fast as he could down the road. Penny was speechless. She really was a witch. Aunt Maggie cackled again and said, "Now then, this magic potion will turn anything back into its original form. I put it in a spray bottle because it will be easier to administer to all the villagers, plus it's much more fun that way."

Penny stared blankly at the witch.

"The fortune was a freebie, but this will cost you. Five gold pieces."

Penny turned out her pockets in the hope of finding something. The same button from earlier popped out and rolled to the ground.

"No money, no sale." The witch pulled a lever, and the

stall transformed back into a cart, which she continued to pull down the road.

"Please, you must help me!"

"I ain't a charity, my dear. I can't go giving my merchandise away. It'll ruin my reputation."

"My friend will die."

"Not my problem."

"But Mr Fitz will never leave our town if we don't defeat him."

The witch stopped. She put down the cart and turned to Penny. "Did you say, Mr Fitz?"

"Yes. He came to our town, selling his phoney formula. Then I accidentally turned him into a dragon, and now he has taken over the village. Please, please help us."

The look on the witch's face made Penny realise she, too, had met Mr Fitz. The wrinkles on her forehead doubled and turned red as she scowled at his name. She looked as though she was about to lay an egg. "Why, that double-crossing, dirty-yarn-spinning, good-for-nothing scoundrel."

"Yep, that's him."

"He sold me a box of what he said were a thousand eyelashes from a thousand lovebirds. They are an extremely expensive and powerful ingredient for making love potions, and he sold them to me at a bargain price. Turned out to be a box of cut-up horsehair. That rotten, black-hearted fibster robbed me of a week's income." She threw the magic potion to Penny. "Take it."

"Wow, thanks, Aunt Maggie."

"And promise me you'll give Mr Fitz a kick up the

backside from me."

"I will," shouted Penny as she ran back where she had come from. Towards Sandwich and towards the battle.

18

HIBERNATION IS OVERRATED

Terrence the gorilla stood perfectly still, blocking the entrance to Sandwich Church. His dark sunglasses glinted in the sun, and his glorious black fur rippled in the wind. He looked magnificent. See for yourself:

- Ten times stronger than the average human.
- The bite force of two lions.
- Weight: 200 kg.
- Arm span: 2.5 m.
- Eats 20 kg of food per day.
- Hair everywhere, even the back of the knees.

As you can see, he was the perfect bodyguard. Nothing

could get past him, except maybe the creature approaching him.

"Grrrrrrrr," growled the creature.

"Excuse me. Did you say something?"

"My head, I have an awful headache. It feels like an axe is sticking out of my skull. Do you have any aspirin?"

"No, but even if I did, I couldn't open them." He wiggled his chubby gorilla fingers. "No opposable thumbs."

The creature looked at where her hands used to be. "Ah yes, we're all animals now. And how on earth did that happen?"

Terrence looked at the creature with suspicion. "Where have you been for the past few months? Hiding under a rock?"

"No. Hibernating under a duvet." The grizzly bear attempted to flatten a large lump of brown hair that was

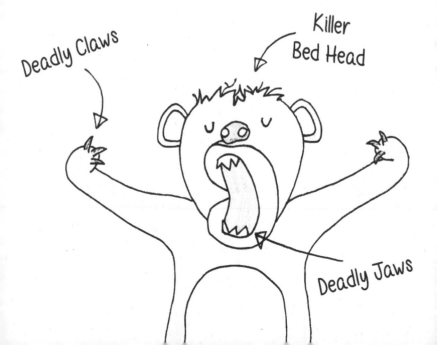

Deadly Claws

Killer
Bed Head

Deadly Jaws

sticking up. "Hibernation has given me killer bedhead and an even worse headache. Something must have woken me up early."

"Ah yes, that'll be our dragon overlord I'm tasked with guarding." Terrence unfolded his arms and pointed behind him. "He's the one who turned the town into a zoo and enslaved us all and right now sounds pretty mad about Earl and Penny's failed plan."

"What!" The grizzly bear was enraged by what she had just heard.

"I know, it's terrible. Fortunately, Penny and Earl were smart enough not to drink that blasted formula, so they're still normal. They've searched high and low to find a knight called George, and they –" Terrence paused to choose his next words carefully "– tried their best."

The grizzly bear – or should I say, Housemistress Lucinda – saw it very differently. "How dare that good-for-nothing, insubordinate little rat disobey me!" She stood on her hind legs and roared as ferociously as a lion who has just discovered there were no more Frosties left.

"I knew it. I knew that naughty child would create total pandemonium if she was allowed outside to rejoin society, and now my worst nightmares have come true. She's turned this town upside down. And don't get me started with that lazy, down-and-out bum."

Terrence disagreed. "Weren't you listening? The one to blame is Mr Fitz, not Penny."

Housemistress Lucinda wasn't listening. It's very difficult to hear when steam is shooting out of your ears in sheer rage.

"And if you ask me, Penny is a very valuable member of this animal kingdom. She's brave and kind and deserves your respect."

Housemistress Lucinda still wasn't listening. This time it was because she had backed up by ten metres, preparing to charge in sheer, uncontrollable rage.

"In fact, over the past month, while you've been asleep, she's done a lot of good stuff. From making hundreds of lasagnes to rallying the townsfolk behind her plan to risking her life to save us all. Without her help, Sandwich would be far worse off. So you should stop punishing Penny and start trusting her."

Housemistress Lucinda didn't get to hear that beautiful speech. This time it was because the one-hundred-and-fifty-kilogram grizzly bear full of sheer, uncontrollable, merciless rage charged into Terrence before he could even start.

19

WHAT ANIMAL WOULD YOU TURN INTO?

The average horseradish grows to around thirty centimetres high, with the size, weight and intelligence of a fat squirrel.

Dragons, on the other hand, can grow to around one thousand centimetres high. They are the size, weight and intelligence of a very fat whale who enjoys really difficult crossword puzzles. It would be like you or me attempting to sink a massive battleship by kicking it. Even the dragon's littlest claw was bigger than the vegetable knights. I know this to be true, because that was what the Four Horseradishes of the Apostrophe were currently under.

"That's a dragon?" cried out Ge, Or, Gi and Na in one voice.

"Yep," shouted Earl, who was hiding behind a charred church pew. "Did I forget to mention the big, sharp claws?"

"Yes, and you could have warned us that the beast has no honour."

"Oh, really?" said the dragon, who had clearly enjoyed the "battle" and was savouring his victory. "How so?"

"You are a cheater," said Ge. "Or you do not understand the rules of rock, paper, scissors."

"I disagree. Did you not see me throw the boulder at you, and my attempts to cut you in two with my claws and rip you to shreds with my teeth?"

"Rock, paper, scissors is a non-combat sport."

"Shame. I much prefer my version of the game. Don't you?"

The horseradish replied with yelps of agony as the dragon dug his claws in deeper.

"I'm glad you agree." The dragon noticed something moving at the back of the church. That was one of the many great things about being a dragon. He had exceptional vision. Nothing could ever slip past him. "So nice of you to join us, traitor."

Penny froze. She clutched the potion in her hand tightly. Maybe he was talking to someone else. Perhaps another traitor had just walked in through the front door.

"I know it's you, Penny."

Penny cursed under her breath. (It was that one adults say when they miss a nail and hit their thumb with a hammer.)

"You might as well come out and explain why you

tried to have me assassinated by these feeble, shrivelled vegetables."

Penny hid the potion spray behind her back and stepped out into the aisle. The church was now completely unrecognisable, and not in a good way. It was such a tip that it made a teenager's bedroom look like a five-star hotel. She reluctantly walked forward, one slow step at a time.

"Believe me, this wasn't how I imagined it would go."

The dragon's spiky eyebrow rose in curiosity. "And how exactly did you imagine it would go, little girl?"

"Well, I wanted to find a George," she said as she cautiously walked towards her target. "You know, a gallant and brave knight in shining armour. But we had to settle for Georgina instead."

"Hey, it's not their fault that Mr Fitz cheated," protested Earl.

SILENCE YOU FOOL!

roared the dragon, leaving a trail of fire. A ball of flame erupted as Earl cartwheeled away just in time.

"No, don't take it out on him," she protested as she continued to creep closer and closer. "Or the vegetables. It's me you should punish. It was my idea, and I alone am responsible."

She was now halfway down the church aisle. There was no turning back now. The dragon flicked the horseradishes down the aisle and reached out towards the girl.

"You were always the clever one," said the dragon as he grabbed Penny and lifted her into the air. "You weren't fooled by my formula. You tricked me into drinking my own devious product. You drugged me with sleeping pills, and you've worked out that only a knight called George can defeat a dragon."

Penny squirmed and just managed to free the hand that was holding the magic spray. She was not close enough, so she stalled by asking the first thing that popped into her head. "What animal do you think I would have turned into if I had drunk your formula?"

"A snake, of course. Probably one of those small, slippery ones that are highly venomous. But I suppose we'll never know." He stopped lifting her up, as she was directly in front of his mouth. He took in a deep breath to prepare for the killing blow.

"I disagree," interrupted Penny.

"What?" said the dragon, intrigued by what she had to say.

"Snakes are dragons without wings or arms or legs, no? I think I would have turned into a skunk."

The dragon laughed a deep belly laugh. "How so?"

"Well, they are little and cute and super adorable. But you don't mess with skunks. You see, when they are cornered and seem utterly defenceless and have no means of escape, that is when they show predators like you exactly what they are capable of."

She grinned, then unleashed the magic spray. It was a direct hit. A cloud of red vapour suffocated the dragon. It even went up his nostrils.

Mr Fitz coughed and spluttered, and as the penny dropped, he dropped Penny.

20

AN
UNEXPECTED GUEST

Water runs.
Leaves fall.

Squirrels scamper.

Dads scratch (either their chins or their backsides, sometimes both at the same time).

Pennies roll . . . but not this Penny. She sprinted as fast as she could towards the exit.

"Don't forget us!" yelled Na. She scooped up the defeated knights and tucked them into her jumper. They clung on to their new, hastier steed with all their roots. Earl already had a head start, but Penny quickly caught up on account of his rotten leg.

ROOOO A A A A ARRR

A vengeful heat erupted behind them. Screams of pain and screeches of agony echoed all around the escapees. There was no time to look back. They were almost at the exit and to safety. Suddenly the doorway blackened, and they bumped head first into the closed doors.

"Quickly," shouted Ge. "Open the door so we may continue our courageous and brave retreat."

"I can't find the handle!" panicked Penny. "What kind of door doesn't have a door handle?"

Earl brushed his hand over the surface. "I reckon if we shave the door, we could find it."

Being a horseradish who lived in the woods, Ge, and his fellow knights, had not encountered a door before. He jumped out of Penny's pockets and chipped in to the urgent discussion. "Perhaps you have to jump on this big paw and twist that sharp tooth at the same time to gain safe passage through the hairy abyss."

Suddenly the furry door crouched down and entered the church. It yawned loudly, then stretched its arms and stamped its feet.

"This door you speak of," said Or, "looks very similar to a bear."

Penny ushered everyone backwards as the big grizzly bear walked on all four paws towards them. She looked into the bear's angry eyes and instantly recognised them.

"There you are, you foul, nasty, wretched little girl." The voice of Housemistress Lucinda, the orphanage housemistress, boomed out of the massive creature. Drool dripped from her pointy teeth as she padded onward. Having slept for a whole month, her housemistress had chronic bedhead. Her breath smelt of a thousand rotten mornings.

"I should have listened. My parents, my friends and my secondary school teacher all warned me. They said, 'Lucinda, never work with children,' and they were right. You've turned all the villagers into animals. You've destroyed the whole town. You've driven me into madness. You should be locked up for the rest of your miserable life."

Penny could find no words. Earl was speechless, for a change. The Four Horseradishes of the Apostrophe watched in

107

terrified silence. Backwards currently seemed like the safest option.

"Young lady, you are *grounded*. Forever and ever, amen. And what I mean by that is I'm going to throw you into a hole in the ground, cover it with dirt and dance until dawn. A naughty girl like you is good for nothing except worm food."

Earl stumbled. Penny fell over. The horseradishes tumbled to the floor. The bear stood on her hind legs and flashed her sharper-than-steel claws.

That was when Buster leaped at the attacker. He had run into the church, seen his friends in danger and bravely rushed to their aid. He flew through the air, teeth and claws out, in an attempt to save Penny. Like a fly swatter, the grizzly bear swung and batted the attack away with one effortless strike. Buster hit a pew and rolled to the floor. He whimpered and whined in agony.

"Buster!" cried Penny.

"Pathetic," heckled the housemistress. "I never liked pets." She took another step closer. "On second thoughts, seeing as you turned me into a bear, maybe I should eat you instead. Yes, very poetic, don't you think? The orphan becomes the food. Hibernation is hungry work."

The bear growled, then slashed her claws towards Penny.

The bear missed.

Bears never usually miss. They are actually extremely talented at mauling defenceless humans. No. It was because a mighty column of fire swallowed the bear up. When the fire stopped, all that was left of her housemistress was a blackened stain on the stone floor. She was gone – poof! – forever and ever, amen.

"Well," said Mr Fitz, who was clearly still a dragon. "You didn't think I'd let that furball have all the fun, did you?"

21

DRAGON ATTACK

The Dragon Overlord of Sandwich was still a dragon. Mr Fitz carefully flicked the spray bottle up in the air using his dragon tail and caught it in his wing. He had already herded his prey into the corner, using his scalding hot fire breath as encouragement, and was now inspecting the potion that was meant to destroy him.

"Hmm, there's something familiar about this potion," said the dragon. He clenched it with his claws and aimed at them. Penny, Earl and the horseradishes huddled together for safety. The dragon squeezed the trigger. A red mist covered them.

The dragon smiled and said, "Is it just me, or does it taste like strawberry-flavoured juice?"

"Screw a light bulb in me ear, paint me white, and call me a lighthouse! It does taste like strawberry-flavoured juice." Earl rather liked it. He would have asked for another spray if someone else had been holding the bottle.

"But . . . b-but," stuttered Penny. "Aunt Maggie said it would turn you back into a human."

"Oh dear, clever girl. Not as smart as I feared," chuckled the dragon. "Haven't you realised yet? People like us like to think anything's for sale."

"Pardon?"

"She's a con woman."

Penny's jaw dropped.

"That's right. I learned everything I know from Aunt Maggie. Oh, so many fond memories of fooling simpletons and scamming villagers. Did she by any chance have a young boy with her?"

"You mean the mushroom?"

"Yes. I used to be that boy. I was a fine apprentice and a very good mushroom, if I say so myself. It's good to hear she's still in the business and hasn't fizzled out."

Penny's whole body deflated. She had been hoodwinked, bamboozled and flimflammed by none other than Mr Fitz's mentor. It was very depressing to think that what she had thought was a magic potion was in fact a fruity drink.

Earl did the gentlemanly thing and lifted Penny's lower jaw back into its normal position. Buster had managed to hobble over and rested his head on her lap. Earl attempted to comfort his friend. "Don't feel bad, Penny. At least you tried your best, and that's the important thing."

"Thanks, Earl," she replied with an added hand on his shoulder.

"You have proven yourself to be a true knight, brave girl," said Ge. "You have looked evil in the eye and decided to face it. You battled the monstrous and dishonourable beast with courage and selflessness. You wrestled with the devil's pet lizard, and—"

"Excuse me," the dragon butted in. "I am right here, you know, and about ten seconds away from incinerating you."

Ge ignored him and continued. "You are truly a brave girl. We would be honoured if you would join us as our fifth Knight of the Woodlands."

"Well, I don't know what to say," said Penny with a wobble of gratitude in her voice. She patted Buster on the head and said, "You are all wonderful friends."

"How about 'I'd like my horseradish well done'?"

"Shh," shushed Earl. "You are interrupting something very special."

The dragon had now well and truly lost his patience. He launched the strawberry potion above the impromptu knighting ceremony and breathed the hottest, reddest flames he could. Nothing was left.

"May I remind you that you double-crossed me?" The enraged dragon took a step forward. "And may I also remind you that I don't like it when my subjects double-cross me?" He took another menacing step forward. "And may I also remind you that I take great pleasure in turning anyone who double-crosses me into ash?"

Penny, Earl, Buster and the horseradishes cowered in the corner. They sensed that this was it.

The end.

"Seeing as your plan has failed, I'll get on with it. Unless somewhere in that pathetic huddle you are hiding a knight called George with a sword worthy of slaying a dragon?"

Suddenly Earl stood up. He had a strange feeling in his head, which a scientist would call brain activity. This strange feeling then compelled him to walk towards his impending doom and speak to his executioner.

"I just remembered something."

"Earl," hissed Penny. "What are you doing? Come back here at once."

"But I've got something to say."

The dragon chuckled. He was clearly amused by Earl's sudden epiphany. "Go on, peasant. You may have your final words."

Earl faced the dragon, took a deep breath and spoke from the brain. "My real name is George."

22

GEORGE
EARL OF SANDWICH

The stone walls of the church wobbled, and so did the stone floor. All the spiders living in the roof who had survived this far were now deaf as well as homeless. (You'll be happy to know that it wasn't all bad for the little creatures, as the heat had turned the church into a lovely sauna.) Sweat dripped down Penny's face as she watched her friend struggle to keep his footing.

Although it may have seemed like it, the dragon was not preparing to attack.

Mr Fitz was laughing.

It was the loudest, longest and largest laugh ever to be recorded in the history books. Imagine one million people all watching the YouTube video of a baby panda sneezing, and you will begin to understand the sheer magnitude of the laugh. The dragon wiped his tearful eyes with his tail and said, "I think I just cracked a rib laughing so hard."

"So, all is forgiven?" asked Penny hopefully.

"Nope. But if I was a more merciful dragon overlord, I would not roast you alive and instead appoint you all as my new jesters."

"I ain't telling no joke," said Earl with his hands on his hips. "It is true. I am called George, and I want to give this knight thing a try."

"Poppycock!" roared the dragon.

"I can prove it too, if you'd kindly delay roasting us alive by a few minutes."

The dragon sat down. The shudder made Penny and the horseradishes bounce into the air. "This should be very entertaining." The dragon smirked. "Please, prove to me you are the one who will defeat me."

Earl set to work searching for something on his person. You see, one of the many difficulties with being homeless was keeping your belongings safe. Peasants do not have wallets or safety deposit boxes or even functioning pockets (and by that, I mean pockets that do not have a hole at the bottom). Fortunately, Earl was creative with where he kept the things most precious to him. He pulled a crumbled piece of paper out from his underarm, smoothed it down and passed it to Penny.

"Do I have to read it?" asked Penny, holding her nose.

"Afraid so. I can't read."

Penny took the corner with the least amount of stains. She immediately noticed lots of fancy words and fancy calligraphy and a very fancy crest at the bottom. She began reading the document from the top.

"It's your birth certificate," announced Penny. "It says here that your full name is George Archibald Percival Egbert Hugo Theodore Sandwich. But I thought your first name was Earl?"

"It's a family nickname. We're all called Earl," said Earl – I mean, George. "I think you'll all agree that it's much easier than calling me by my full name. You see, a long time ago, my ancestors didn't just own the big mansion my friend Penny lives in, they owned the whole of Sandwich."

Everyone gasped. Not only was Earl called George, but he was also the long-lost ancestor of the Earl of Sandwich, and the rightful heir to his estate. The peasant with no home was in fact the wealthiest man in the whole of England.

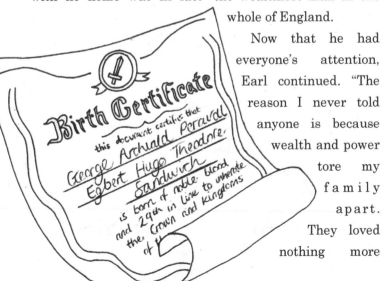

Now that he had everyone's attention, Earl continued. "The reason I never told anyone is because wealth and power tore my family apart. They loved nothing more than increasing taxes and mocking the penniless. When my parents died, I swore I would never be like them. In fact, I wanted to be their opposite – poor in money but rich in friends – until now. If reclaiming my title means I can save our village, then so be it."

The dragon clapped. Not in the normal way humans clap, because he had tiny arms. He slammed his tail down and up and down again. "Well done, I'll give you that. You are called George, even if it's one of your many stupid middle names. But that does not make you a knight. You must have noble blood and be of noble birth. Look at you," sniggered the dragon. "You are a peasant, and no piece of paper can change that."

"Don't let the beast talk to you like that, Earl," shouted Or.

"Break his snout and gallop on his tail," added Na.

Earl neighed. He wasn't sure why. He just felt that it was the most appropriate thing he could do in this situation. He was a noble steed, but how could he prove to the dragon he had noble blood? Suddenly it became as clear as fresh mud in Earl's simple mind. He ripped off his trousers, unstrapped something from his rotten leg, nicked his finger with the tip and held out his bleeding finger towards the dragon.

"Here you go."

The dragon was speechless. So was everyone else. Standing in his underpants, Earl turned to Penny and said, "I ain't sure how we are going to check my blood. Fingers criss-crossed there is some of that nobility stuff in there."

"Earl?"

"Yes, me dear."

"What is that you had strapped to your leg and are now holding in your hand?" asked Penny.

"Oh, this old thing?" He swished it about a bit. "Family heirloom. Been passed down from Earl to Earl for generations. Before my dad died, he gave it to me and said, 'Earl, this thing is very important. Our family has got an important job to do. When the time comes, you'll know what to do with it.' I reckon that time is now. It made a lovely little cut. Look, blood is pouring out of my finger like it's a gravy boat."

The dragon slowly backed away. He did not want to get too close to the thing. You see, Mr Fitz had instantly recognised it.

It was pointy.

It was shiny.

It was long and heavy-looking.

It was jewel-encrusted at the hilt.

It was sharp on both edges (and especially sharp at the pointy end).

All in all, it was a magnificent sword.

Earl was currently leaning on his sword like it was a walking stick. "We'll just have to postpone our big fisticuffs, Mr Fitz, until my blood test comes back."

"But, Earl," shouted all four vegetables and Penny. "You are a knight!"

"Really?" questioned Earl. Remember, he was very much used to being called a peasant by everyone, so this was going to take some convincing. "How can you be so sure?"

"Your name is George," said Ge.

"You have a sword passed down through your family," said Or.

"You are a natural steed," said Gi.

"More than a natural," added Na. "You are truly a *noble* steed."

"Bark!" barked Buster encouragingly.

"Plus it says so on your birth certificate." Penny joined Earl and pointed at the words at the bottom of the official document as she read aloud. "'Let this document show that George Archibald Percival Egbert Hugo Theodore Sandwich is a direct descendant of the English nobility and therefore a Knight of the Realm."

"Cover me in tin foil and call me a knight! I am a knight!"

"Ah," butted in a nervous-sounding dragon. "So, you have a fancy birth certificate and a shiny sword and have descended from nobility, but do you have the birthmark in the shape of a frying pan on your bottom? The one that legend foretells the knight who would slay the Dragon of Sandwich would have."

As we have all discovered, Earl needed no encouragement in this department. He dropped his pants and proudly pointed to his left butt cheek.

"Oh, drat," whined the dragon. "But I made that one up."

23

FIGHT!

A Knight of the Realm, who is of noble blood and has chosen the noble profession, will spend around ten years in training. To be clear, we are talking about human knights and not vegetable knights.

They are taught how to do the following:

- fight
- win jousting tournaments
- ride a noble steed
- wear steel plate armour
- look down their noses at peasants
- kiss the hand of a princess
- and most importantly, how to defeat a dragon.

Less than half of the students pass the final exam (because it involves completing the Gauntlet of Death, immediately followed by the Gauntlet of Eternal Suffering, immediately followed by a cup of tea and a ginger biscuit, immediately followed by the Gauntlet of the Self-Assessment Tax Return). Then, after graduation, many fail to make it back for the one-year reunion party. The life of a knight is extremely perilous. The only profession that has a higher mortality rate is crocodile dentist.

Earl had been a knight for a little over thirty seconds.

The very first thing he did after learning he was a knight was pull down his underpants and show his bottom to a dragon. If he had completed the ten-year knight training course, he would know not to do this. It's actually one of the first things you learn, along with "never tease a dragon".

"Ha ha de ha ha!" sang Earl at the top of his voice as he danced around the church. "Look at me! I'm the one who is going to slay you, Mr Big-Scaredy-Cat Dragon, and I've got the frying pan birthmark to prove it."

The dragon had now retreated to the bell tower. Mr Fitz knew that ancient stories and mythical prophecies were not to be trifled with. From his vantage point, he belched fireball after fireball after fireball at his enemies. Penny, Earl, Buster and the four horseradishes were in trouble.

The flames engulfed them.

The smoke suffocated them.

The heat scalded them.

But hope propelled them.

"Brave girl," shouted Ge as he dodged the dancing

flames. "Put me on the dog's back, and I will play my part with honour."

"But you'll never make it!"

"Answer me this: do you believe the peasant can defeat the dragon?"

"No," said Penny without hesitation. They looked at Buster for a third opinion. The dog shook his head and readied himself for the final charge.

Ge patted Buster's paw and said, "Earl needs our help. He needs your steadfast bravery, Buster's nimble agility and my foolish courage. Quickly, we are losing precious time."

Penny caught sight of something glinting in Ge's hand. Then she understood. She picked up Ge and placed him on Buster's back. The dog galloped through the church like the noblest of steeds, narrowly dodging several fireballs. Somehow Buster managed to reach the bell tower without a single singed hair. The dragon was clearly spooked. He had never missed a moving target before now.

Ge tugged on Buster's ear and pointed at the rope. Buster tugged on the rope and looked up at the church bell. The bell swung and loudly rang directly in the dragon's ear. The dragon clutched his ringing ear and fell to the ground with a thud. The horseradish jumped onto the dragon's forehead and rolled down his eyelid. Ge closed his tiny eyes, held the cheese grater tightly and began to grate himself.

Bits of horseradish began to fall into the dragon's eyes, which instantly turned red and bloodshot. The pain Mr

Fitz felt was like wearing glasses made of chopped onions, thorns and super red-hot chilli powder. He squealed in anguish.

"Now, Earl!" shouted Penny. "Now's your chance."

The knight had been hiding under a pile of scorched hymnbooks. Earl heard the command and leaped into action. He galloped with his arm outstretched and his eyes closed. Nothing could stop him from his destiny and his predestined victory. Except, say, if he had forgotten something.

"Earl, where is the sword?"

He skidded to a halt and opened his eyes. "Fiddlesticks. I thought this felt a bit on the light side." He threw the stick with a marshmallow on the end to one side for later.

"I may have been blinded and deafened, Sir Earl of Sandwich, but I can still smell the stench rising from the filth under your toenails." The mighty tail of the dragon swung into the unprepared knight and catapulted him into the air. Earl hit the stone wall and collapsed to the ground.

Penny rushed over to her friend, dragging his sword behind her. Buster stood in front of them and growled at the dragon, guarding them with his life. Penny hugged Earl with all her being. She felt him breathing, weakly, and thanked the heavens he had survived.

"Who could possibly think," continued the dragon, "that he could ever defeat me? I would bet my entire pile of gold and win every time. And now I'll finish this absurdity once and for all."

She closed her eyes tight as she felt the enormous intake

of breath. She squeezed her friend tighter as the dragon's lungs reached full capacity. She said a prayer in the pause before the end.

Then came something highly unexpected.

CHARGE!

The horseradishes charged, and it was a really, really good charge. Nothing like all their previous attempts. That was because they had help, and a lot of it. All of the villagers joined them as they stampeded into the church. They had no weapons to charge with and no hands to hold them in. However, they did have something else, and they had it in abundance . . . **POO**.

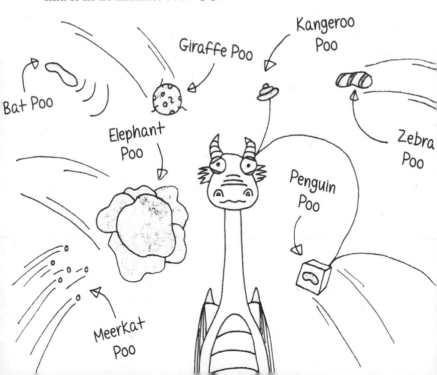

Kangeroo Poo

Giraffe Poo

Bat Poo

Elephant Poo

Zebra Poo

Penguin Poo

Meerkat Poo

Zebra poo.

Meerkat poo.

Chinchilla poo (which made very good pellets for Reverend Nightingale's pea-shooter).

Reindeer poo.

Giraffe poo.

Penguin poo (which takes three to four days to defrost, but Mrs Wrinklebottom had used the defrost setting in her shop's microwave).

Kangaroo poo.

Bat poo.

Elephant poo (which was being brought in using wheelbarrows and thrown like snowballs by Terrence and Mr Dickens and many, many other villagers).

Never had a church building ever been as whiffy as this one. Mr Fitz was covered from tail to snout in all kinds and varieties and specimens of the icky stuff. Now he had lost his hearing, his sight and his smell.

Penny helped Earl to his feet, passed him the sword and said, "Time to fulfil your destiny."

24

HAVE MERCY

Earl ached all over.

He had bruises on top of his bruises.

He felt strangely light-headed and carefree (which in the medical profession is called concussed). To look at him, stumbling down the aisle towards his foe, you would think the knight had never held a sword before. If you have ever played pin the tail on the donkey, you'll know what I mean.

Mr Fitz was down. He was, as they say, a sitting duck.

The time to strike was now.

Earl struck.

The sound of metal on stone screeched through the church.

"That was the baptismal font," shouted Penny. "Try

again."

Earl struck again.

"Closer. A little to the left this time."

Earl struck for a third time. This time the pained howl of a dragon filled the rafters like a choir of middle-aged men standing on little pieces of Lego. Penny, the horseradishes and all the villagers burst into wild and joyous applause. Buster woofed with delight.

It was a direct hit. Mr Fitz yelped and cried and screamed as the sword plunged deep into his right buttock. Earl had managed to stick the sword in close to the dragon's tail. He might not have been especially talented at being a knight, but it turned out he was very good at party games.

The dragon, who now had a sword sticking out of his butt, stumbled around the church. The roars of agony made the walls shake and floor shudder twice as much as his snoring. He tried everything to remove the sword. He reached with his tiny hands and flicked his tail and twisted his long neck, but nothing worked.

He needed help. He needed a friend.

He looked around the room. All of his enslaved subjects surrounded him. Tears streamed down his scaly cheeks, but nobody reached for the tissues. Everyone was still clapping and cheering at his defeat. Some were even pointing at the sword and laughing. Mr Fitz realised something. He did not have any friends.

Penny stepped forward, closely followed by Sir George Archibald what's-his-face Egbert some-other-posh-sounding-names Sandwich.

"It's time to end this," shouted Terrence, the gorilla blacksmith. "Go on, Earl. You remember how the storybook ends."

"Please," pleaded Mr Fitz. "Have mercy! Have mercy! I was never going to kill anyone, except for that awful old hag. Did you hear what she said? She wanted to lock Penny up in that orphanage and throw away the key. I couldn't let her do that, because . . . well . . ." He paused to find some courage to say the next sentence. He was about to reveal something that conmen should never, ever say. "I've grown to like you all."

"Don't listen to him, Earl. How can we trust the words of a con man?" shouted Mr Dickens, the lion dentist.

"This is embarrassing to admit," confessed Mr Fitz, "but I must tell you the truth. Being a travelling con man sucks. You can never stay in one place for too long, until now. At first I enslaved you all to make me feel important and feed me lasagne, but after a while, I started to see how everyone in this village knew each other's names and said nice things to each other and didn't eat each other, even though you all look extremely tasty. I've grown to care about the same people I imprisoned. And if you can forgive me, I'd like to join your village community."

"How can you expect us to forgive you after everything you've done?" said Reverend Nightingale, the mouse vicar. "Look at us. We're all creatures great and small."

"I'll repair what I have destroyed, and I'll rebuild what I've destroyed." The dragon reached into a concealed pouch in his belly and revealed a spray bottle. "And as for turning you into animals, here, it's the real antidote."

"Poppycock," scoffed Mrs Wrinklebottom, the zebra sandwich shop owner. "No one can change. You'll always be a liar. Finish this, Earl."

Earl paused. He was thinking, very hard. He had never given his brain such a tough morality workout. Sweat trickled down his forehead, and heat haze rose from his head, and if you listened carefully, you could hear both his brain cells having a heated discussion. Almost a minute passed before Penny stepped in.

"We don't like the storybook ending," announced Penny. "Do we, Earl?"

Earl shook his head. "Nope. It stinks. A story that ends with murder isn't a story I want to be a part of. I much prefer stories that have a happy ending, like true love's kiss or long-lost family being reunited."

Buster jumped and skipped and frolicked at the suggestion. He barked and woofed and howled and yelped in delight.

"Buster, I'm not going to kiss the dragon."

The dragon looked horrified. "That's not what the dog wants." Mr Fitz handed Penny the spray bottle and said, "I think you should be the first one to administer the cure, and you should start with Buster."

"What?" replied Penny. "Don't be stupid."

Buster pawed at Penny's leg and looked into her eyes. She looked into the dog's eyes and knew deep down what she should do next. She took a step back, aimed, then squeezed. A red mist covered the dog. Penny thought it looked the same as before, until something started to happen.

All the dog's hair fell to the ground.

Whiskers retracted and claws shrank and teeth flattened.

The tail disappeared too.

The dog was no longer a dog. Buster was now a human. A man that Penny instantly recognised.

IS THAT YOU DAD?

25

A BRAND NEW SANDWICH

There once was a busy and vibrant village on the south-east coast of England called Sandwich.

The whole of the country read about this strange place in the national newspapers when a dragon was defeated inside the local church. They read about a brave girl and the quirky villagers and how the Earl of Sandwich had saved the day and how a daughter had been reunited with her long-lost father. It was a wonderful read, if I may say so myself.

Nothing used to happen in Sandwich, but now

something happened . . . and
it did so every day, at 7 p.m.
to be precise, according to this
big sign.

> BATTLE RE-ENACTMENT
> AT 19:00 IN
> SANDWICH ZOO
> (PLEASE WEAR FLAME
>   RETARDANT CLOTHING)

A large crowd had gathered
to watch the show. Families
from every corner of the United
Kingdom would travel to Sandwich to see
the show. The murmurings quietened
down as Penny walked across the stage.
She was wearing a top hat and tails, just like a circus
ringmaster.

"Ladies and gentlemen," announced Penny in a grand
announcement voice to the enthralled audience. "Welcome
to Sandwich Zoo. Please remember to wear your flame-
retardant poncho at all times and enjoy the show."

The show began. It was mesmerising.

The dragon roared and spat fire and scared all the
children. The actor who played Earl rode gallantly on
horseback and did some very impressive swordplay. The
smoke machine and green lasers and theatrical music
added to the drama. The crowd clapped and cheered and
loved every second of the exciting theatre production.

Now, if you or I were in the audience, we may have
spotted a few tiny inconsistencies. I do not remember Earl
ever riding a horse. He did enjoy pretending to be one, but
he never did a handstand on a horse as it galloped and
jumped through hoops of fire. I don't remember any of the
villagers breaking into choreographed dance routines and

singing "Lasagne, Glorious Lasagne". The firework display at the end was a spectacular addition and much less messy than all the poo-flinging. Backstage after the show, the cast and crew gathered to discuss the performance.

"Excellent work, everyone," congratulated Penny. "You've earned every clap tonight."

"I think I can do much better," said a young actor in a horseradish costume. "You see, it is extremely challenging to play a talking horseradish when you've never met one before."

"Nonsense. You're a splendid horseradish. Besides, they have more important things to do than give out acting tips." Penny smiled. She thought of the four, well, three and a half Knights of the Woodlands protecting their kingdom and wished they had stayed. Earl had offered them a job protecting his new vegetable patch, but they had said something about sacred oaths and had said their goodbyes.

Mr Fitz lowered his dragon head to join the conversation. "I agree. Your performance brought a tear to my eye."

"Really? Thanks very much. That means a lot coming from someone who witnessed the actual battle."

"Yes, quite," replied Mr Fitz as his eyeball twitched in remembrance of that strange day. "I must say, Penny, I am rather enjoying my community service as an actor and zoo attraction." The dragon yawned from a hard day's work and said, "Being a professional actor is wonderful. In fact, it's much like being a professional con man but without the constant lying and bottling up. Now I know that it was the crowd-gathering I loved the most. Have we had any complaints from the front row tonight?"

"None. Your aim is getting much better."

"Thanks, brave girl." Mr Fitz smiled and winked and headed back to his enclosure. Not many zoos in the country can say they have a dragon, only Sandwich Zoo.

Penny walked over towards her old house. The orphanage looked very different. It looked loved. That was because the Earl of Sandwich had returned and reclaimed all his properties and lands and vast wealth. The earl was at the very top of a ladder, washing a window, when Penny approached the house.

"Good evening, Earl."

"Good evening, Penny."

"You do know you could pay a window cleaner to do that for you."

"I know, but I am a homeowner now, and I want to enjoy every millimetre of it."

"You're not a homeowner, Earl. You're more of a giant-mansion-with-a-zoo-in-the-back-garden-owner."

"Shave me head and call me a baked potato." Earl slid down the ladder on his two perfectly working legs and landed with a thud King Henry the Eighth would have been proud of. "Indeed I am."

Earl had had many wonderful ideas after he had defeated Mr Fitz and saved Sandwich. So many, in fact, I've had to make a list:

1. He inherited the stately home of the original Earl of Sandwich, which used to be the orphanage.
2. He built a zoo in his back garden so that any of the village creatures who had decided to stay as

135

an animal would have a new home.

3. He appointed Penny's dad as the head zookeeper, because he was very good at herding thanks to his lingering canine instincts.
4. He gave Mr Fitz a new job as a tourist attraction.
5. He employed Terrence the blacksmith to forge all the signs, gates, fences and animal enclosures.
6. He gave Mrs Wrinklebottom a generous loan to expand The Sandwich Sandwich Shop to fit in all the tourists.
7. He donated lots and lots of money to rebuild Sandwich Church.
8. Penny was already the happiest girl in the world. She had her dad back, so Earl did nothing for her (well, except for buying her the biggest flat-screen TV in the whole of England).

All in all, everyone loved the Earl of Sandwich, and the Earl of Sandwich loved everyone. He had started out with nothing, and he had finished with everything.

"Goodnight, Penny," said Earl.

"Goodnight, Earl," said Penny.

And with that, the two friends skipped off towards their new homes. Penny stopped outside her house. It was tiny. The front garden was a single paving slab. It had one toilet, two poky bedrooms and no central heating. It did not have any chandeliers or indoor fountains or spiral staircases. None of that mattered to her, because inside was someone waiting to give her a big hug and make her a hot chocolate and ask her how her day had gone.

Penny felt like the richest girl in the world.

SAD THIS BOOK IS OVER???

HERE'S 3 THINGS TO DO NOW...

TRY READING MY LATEST
SERIES – 'THE SUPER NERDS'

FREE EBOOK

CAN THE
SCHOOL NERDS
BECOME THE SCHOOL
SUPERHEROES?

CHECK OUT THE FREE STUFF:

FREE EBOOKS:
- EPISODE ONE IN THE SUPER NERDS
- 49 EXCUSES FOR NOT TIDYING MY BEDROOM
- TRUTH OR POOP? AMAZING ANIMALS

WEBSITE SIGN-UPS:
- THE TRUTH OR POOP FAMILY EMAIL QUIZ
- NEWSLETTER FREEBIES

SCAN ME TO GET
25% OFF
OFF YOUR
FIRST ORDER

OR VISIT WWW.CJWARWOOD.COM
AND ENTER DISCOUNT CODE AMAZING25 AT THE CHECKOUT

ABOUT
THE AUTHOR

James Warwood is a writer and illustrator who lives on the borders of North Wales with his wife, two sons, and cactus (called Steve the Cactus).

He has a degree in Theology, which at the time seemed like a great idea, until he released he didn't want to become an RE Teacher. Instead, he writes laugh-out-loud middle grade fiction and non-fiction. He also fills them with his silly cartoons. He is the bestselling author of the EXCUSE ENCYCLOPEDIA and the TRUTH OR POOP SERIES.

James likes whiskey, squirrels, reading silly books, playing his bass guitar, and Greggs Sausage Rolls. He does not like losing at board games or having to writing about himself in the third person.

OTHER BOOKS BY JAMES WARWOOD

TRUTH OR POOP?

True or false quiz books for the whole family. Learn something new and laugh as you do it!

THE 49 SERIES

Non-fiction cartoon series full of helpful tips and laugh-out-loud silliness for getting the most out of life.

THE SUPER NERDS

Can the school nerds become the school superheroes? Join Reggie and Hilda as they discover the true power of friendship.

Episode One: The Snail Army of Doom

Episode Two: The Golden Sneeze Machine

MIDDLE-GRADE STAND-ALONE FICTION

The Boy Who Stole One Million Socks

The Girl Who Vanquished the Dragon

WHERE TO FIND JAMES ONLINE

Website:

www.cjwarwood.com

Facebook & Instagram:

Search for James Warwood

ORDER BOOKS DIRECT FROM THE AUTHOR

BV - #0175 - 270824 - C0 - 203/127/8 - PB - 9781915646125 - Matt Lamination